Slapshots

DISCARD

All-Mars All-Stars

Look for other books in the Slapshots series

Book #1: The Stars from Mars

All-Mars All-Stars

Gordon Korman

AN
APPLE
PAPERBACK

SCHOLASTIC INC.
New York Toronto London Auckland Sydney
Mexico City New Delhi Hong Kong

ISBN 0-590-70620-9

12 11 10 9 8 7 6 5 4 3 2 1   9/9 0 1 2 3 4/0

Printed in the U.S.A.   40

First Scholastic printing, November 1999

For Jay Howard Korman
Great Star of the 2020s

All-Mars All-Stars

||||| _**Chapter 1**_

STARS FROM MARS CLIMB OUT
OF LAST PLACE

by Clarence "Chipmunk" Adelman,
Gazette Sports Reporter

Even though the city of Waterloo and the town of Mars are only separated by a narrow canal, this is the first season that a team from Mars has been allowed to play in the Waterloo Slapshot League. The Stars had a shaky start, but no one is laughing at them anymore. A win last Saturday improved their record to 3 and 5 and lifted them out of the basement in the standings. . . .

The man finished reading my article and looked up at me. "So?"

"So I'm the official team reporter," I explained. "I have to be right behind the players' bench. You're in my seat."

The man laughed. "Everybody else has a team and a coach and that's it," he said, shoving over to make me some room in the bleachers. "You Martians have to have an official reporter."

He seemed like a pretty nice guy, so I didn't make a big stink about him calling me a Martian. The term is Marser, and all those Waterloo types know it. They always make us feel like second-class citizens.

Jared Enoch, left wing, turned around on the players' bench and spotted me. "It's the third period, Chipmunk! Where have you been?"

"I got detention," I replied unhappily. "Mr. Ping caught me with a jawbreaker in science. I tried to lie, but he pounded me on the back, and it flew out of my mouth and landed in a beaker of acid." I sighed. "I've never seen a sourball disappear so fast."

"Wasn't that your last one?" asked assistant captain Trent Ruben. He was the league MVP and the only Waterloo kid on the Stars.

I nodded sadly. "I could have sucked on that baby for two hours. Instead, it dissolved in two seconds."

"We're on," came a quiet voice.

It was Alexia Colwin, team captain, and the only girl in the Waterloo Slapshot League. Alexia worked

2

on a kind of reverse volume control. The stuff most people shouted came out of her in a soft whisper. She, Trent, and Jared disappeared over the boards and joined the play.

I checked the score. The Stars were tied 6–6 with the Pretty Baby Diaper Service Kings.

I whipped out my reporter's notebook. It was as much a part of me as my writing hand. The Kings had a reputation for running up big numbers. But their defense was weak, so the Stars had been able to match them goal for goal. The Kings had a lot of grade-seven kids from the junior high. Their forwards were taller than the Stars, with long legs that enabled them to skate faster.

A big winger chased down the puck in the corner. He feathered a perfect pass to the Kings' captain, another seventh-grader everyone called King Diaper.

Pow!

King Diaper one-timed a booming slapshot. The Stars' goalie, Josh Colwin, Alexia's twin, went into a split. His sprawling pad made a kick-save as he flopped.

"The thingamajig! Clear the thingamajig!" bellowed the foghorn voice of Coach Boom Boom Bolitsky.

I should really explain about the Stars' coach. He never used any nouns because he could never come

up with the names of stuff. Instead, he called everything a thingamajig, a doohickey, a whatchamacallit — words like that. Language came easy to
Boom Boom. He never used it.

The puck went right to the other winger, but Brian
Azevedo, our defenseman, had him tied up in front
of the net. The bigger King wrestled himself free
from Brian and raised his stick to shoot.

Wham!

Alexia drove her shoulder into his stomach and
put him flat on his back on the ice. By now most of
the teams were used to playing against a girl. The
part that was hard for them to accept was that she
was the toughest checker in the league.

Alexia fed Kyle Ickes, Brian's defense partner.
Kyle started for the neutral zone, grinning his appre-
ciation for the crisp pass.

Right now you're probably asking yourself how
Kyle could be rushing up ice and grinning down ice
at the same time. You see, Kyle skates backwards. I
mean *always*, even when he's going forward. He's
the total opposite of Brian, who can't skate backwards to save his life.

Kyle reversed across the red line. He kept an
eye on where he was going by checking the car
mirror that was superglued to his face mask. When
a Kings' defenseman made a move for the puck,

Kyle executed a perfect deke, all without turning around.

Just before the blue line, he flipped the puck to Trent. I clutched my pencil a little tighter. You don't even have to be much of a hockey fan to love watching Trent Ruben.

He had two men to beat. First he swerved around a body check with the grace of a ballet dancer. Then he turned on the jets and left the other defenseman in a shower of snow. By the time he came in on net, he was flying. He fired a snap shot that was so quick that the puck was in the net before the Kings' goalie even moved.

The Mars fans roared to their feet, applauding the go-ahead goal. I was doing my usual balancing act, trying to cheer and make notes at the same time. This was what being a sportswriter is all about! Oh, sure, I know the *Waterloo Elementary School Gazette* isn't very good. Okay, it's a rag. I wouldn't line a birdcage with it. But this is just a stepping-stone for me. One day, I'm going to be the hockey reporter for *Sports Illustrated.*

Less than two minutes remained in the game. The Kings put together a late surge, and the Stars struggled to hold them off. In the last minute of play, the Kings' goalie golfed a clearing pass that hit a stick and soared high in the air. A gasp went up in the arena. King Diaper was hovering around the red line, waiting for a last-minute breakaway chance. Suddenly, Jared jumped high and reached for the puck with his glove. The rules said he couldn't catch it or knock it to a teammate. His only option was to bat it to the ice at his feet.

The puck glanced off the tips of his fingers, deflected straight up, and then came down. It disappeared inside the neck of his jersey. The whistle blew.

"All right, kid," said the referee. "Give me the puck."

Jared patted himself all over. "It isn't here."

"It's got to be there. I saw it go down your shirt."

The two of them looked. Jared took off his sweater and then his shoulder pads. Both teams went over to help out. They poked, prodded, and searched. No puck.

"Try his whatchamacallit," advised Boom Boom from the bench.

By this time, titters of laughter were spreading through the crowd like measles.

"It's not funny, you know!" Jared howled at the stands.

This provoked belly laughs.

"It must be in your pants," decided the linesman.

"I'm not taking off my pants!" Jared raged. "Not unless everybody in the audience turns around!"

The referee glared at Boom Boom. "Will you get him out of here?"

I got a great headline idea: *Mystery Puck Still at Large*.

The game went on with a new puck, but Jared never found the old one.

The Stars held on for a 7–6 victory.

Chapter 2

Since the locker room was coed, the Stars only changed out of their skates and helmets for the ride home. As the team reporter, I went in to report on the celebration.

Boom Boom was pretty happy. "Great thinga-mabob!" he roared, slapping players on the back.

Josh threw down his goalie mask and began pounding the snow off his pads with his stick. "What a rush!" he exclaimed to Trent. "Your stick-handling is like magic! You faked those guys right out of their diapers!"

Cal Torelli brayed a laugh, donkey-style. "Out of their diapers! I get it! Because they're sponsored by a diaper service!"

It didn't take much to amuse Cal. Knock-knock

jokes made him absolutely hysterical. Road Runner cartoons practically put him in intensive care.

The locker room door opened, and in came the coach's wife with the team's post-game snack. This was always something gross, like organic wheat germ alfalfa junk. The Bolitskys ran Mars Health Food, which was also the team sponsor.

"Congratulations, everybody!" beamed Mrs. B., handing out multigrain spinach crisps and power shakes. It was a secret Stars' rule that no one was allowed to tell the Bolitskys how bad their food was.

Even though I wasn't officially on the team, I was not excused from the torture.

I had a system for keeping my mind off the terrible taste of this stuff. I just kept looking at Mrs. Bolitsky.

Put it this way: Our Mrs. B. was gorgeous enough to stop traffic. Movie stars looked like baboons next to her. Most of the guys were doing the same as me — staring. She was six feet tall, with long black hair, and eyes that — forget it. You'd have to be Shakespeare to describe this lady. I could write about a five-on-three power play better than him, but I don't have the words for Mrs. B. There might not be any.

We called the Bolitskys Beauty and the Beast, so

you know which part that left for Boom Boom. He was tall, scrawny, and bug-eyed, with a crooked nose and missing teeth. Those were the trophies of his sixteen-year NHL career as a player nobody ever heard of. The crown of his head was as bald as a cue ball. But in the back, he had long frizzy hair tied in a ponytail. He was a mutt, no question about it. He was also the nicest guy in the world and a first-class coach.

Since Mrs. B. was present, Alexia was the only Star who could speak. "Great milk shake, Mrs. Bolitsky."

"Oh, it's not a *milk* shake," she replied. "It's completely nondairy. It's made with soybean extract and flavored with mashed kiwi fruit."

Like we needed to know that.

I decided it was time to get a little reporter's business done.

"How does it feel to be four and five?" I asked everyone.

Alexia grinned. "Considering they expected us to wash out of the league a month ago, it feels pretty good."

"Do you realize we're only one game away from an even win-lose record?" added Josh excitedly.

"That's five-hundred hockey!" I exclaimed, scribbling at top speed. "After starting out oh and three, to be at five hundred by the All-Star Tournament would be Cinderella stuff!"

Boom Boom lifted his head out of the equipment bag. "Five-hundred hockey is fine. But the important whatsit is to play our best every thingamabob, and take it one heejazz at a time."

"Boom Boom always says that," confirmed Mrs. Bolitsky.

Always says *what*?

That was life in the Stars' locker room. A lot of great wisdom was probably flying around. But you needed a translator to understand it.

Trent lived near the Waterloo community center, where the league played its games. So he could walk home. The rest of us took the two-mile drive back to Mars in the team "bus." This was actually the ancient rust-bucket of a delivery truck from Mars Health Food, the Bolitskys' store and restaurant. Remember the rearview mirror on Kyle's face guard? It fell off this truck. I'm amazed the tires, fenders, bumpers, and motor didn't do the same.

So you can imagine how comfortable it was for ten kids and tons of hockey gear to rattle over the bridge, trying not to bounce off giant plastic tubs of tofu.

My mom was waiting for me just inside the door. I was expecting her to pat me down and search my book bag for jawbreakers — I had eleven cavities at my last dental checkup. But that wasn't what was up.

"We have a visitor, Clarence," she told me.

Why do I like being called Chipmunk? Because anything is better than Clarence.

Then a familiar voice said, "Hey, buddy." Out of the living room stepped my father.

"Dad!" I ran over and hugged him.

I didn't get a chance to see him that much. That wasn't really his fault. He was a salesman, which meant he had to travel a lot. My parents split up when I was seven.

"It's good to see you, Chipmunk," he told me with a big grin.

I felt my mother wince. "Mitch, *please* don't call him that!" she begged. "That nickname comes from the way his cheek is all puffed out when he's eating jawbreakers! We're having nightmare dental problems here!"

I know when it's time to change the subject. "So, Dad, are you still selling that new computer gizmo?"

He laughed. "Gizmo?"

"Gizmo, heejazz, doojig, whatsit. They're Boom Boom Bolitsky words. He's the coach of the Stars.

Did you know that we have a team in the Waterloo League?"

He nodded. "So your mom's been telling me. It's a miracle! We've been trying to pull that off since *I* was a kid! I'd really love to see your writing on the team. Do you keep a scrapbook?"

Did I keep a scrapbook! I had every word I'd ever published in the *Gazette* lovingly pasted and preserved up in my room. Of course, I had cut out the part that said *Waterloo Elementary School Gazette* and glued in the cover logo of *Sports Illustrated*.

Dad scanned my first two articles. "This is terrific stuff! Congratulations, Chipmunk. Oh, by the way —" From his pocket he produced a small cellophane-wrapped package and handed it to me.

I grinned. It was a Grape-ola Mega-Bomb, one of my favorite jawbreakers. It had real fruit-juice explosions inside.

"Thanks, Dad!"

"At your service." He winked. "Just don't tell Mom it came from me."

I made a face. "Are you kidding? If she catches me with one more jawbreaker, I won't live long enough to report on the Stars' next practice — and that's tomorrow!"

"Tomorrow?" Dad zoomed right in on the information. "Here in Mars? I should be through with my appointments in time to catch an after-school practice."

"*Really*?" I was psyched. "Are you in town for a long time?"

"Could be a few weeks," he replied. "Listen, Chipmunk, I should get back to my hotel. I'll see you at the rink tomorrow, okay?"

"Good night, Dad." I hugged him again, and off he went.

Listen, I'm not one of those kids who spends all his time wishing and hoping and praying for his parents to get back together again. My folks seemed to be pretty good friends, and that was okay with me. But I was really excited to have Dad around for a while. Especially since he was interested in the Stars.

I picked up my Grape-ola Mega-Bomb. Mom was nuts when it came to the dentist. She had actually given my school picture to every candy store in Mars so they wouldn't sell to me. That was an extra added bonus of having Dad nearby. I was back on the jaw-breaker gravy train.

⁍⁍⁍⁍⁍ Chapter 3

For some reason, the Waterloo kids thought there was nothing more hilarious than making fun of us Marsers. They called us Martians, and space hicks, and nebula nerds. They even named the school bus Pathfinder after the NASA Mars mission.

The Waterloo adults weren't much better than the kids. They were more polite, maybe, but the jokes were the same.

"We are now entering Earth's atmosphere," announced Mrs. Kolodny, our school bus driver. "Prepare for docking at spaceport Waterloo."

You see? Mrs. Kolodny said that every single day! We were all so sick of it! All except Cal, who thought it was brilliant.

"Earth's atmosphere!" he chortled. "That's a riot!"

"It's been a riot every day since kindergarten,"

snarled Alexia in reverse volume control. "It's not a riot anymore."

There was a big crowd of Waterloo kids hanging around the entrance. They were laughing and joking and having a great time, which usually meant some poor Marser was going to get roasted.

There was a paper taped to the door. I peered over to read it:

THE GREAT MARTIAN PUCK SEARCH

Slowly, we moved inside. There in the foyer was the department store dummy they'd used to humiliate us before. It carried a hockey stick and wore a helmet and a green T-shirt doctored up to look like a Stars jersey — number ten, Jared's number. From the stick dangled another sign:

HELP THIS MARTIAN FIND HIS MISSING PUCK. HINT — IT'S REALLY CLOSE TO HIS BRAIN.

Did I mention that the dummy wasn't wearing any pants? How can I explain where they put the "missing" puck? Let's just say that the dummy would have had a hard time sitting down.

Cal barked a laugh right in Jared's face. "Hey, Jared, did you ever think of looking *there*?"

Jared was fire-engine red. "I never found it!" he complained.

"Have you checked your hockey pants?" Josh suggested. "Maybe it slipped into one of those pockets where the protectors fit."

Jared glared at him. "My mom already washed my hockey pants! She washed all my equipment! There wasn't any puck!"

"Then it must have fallen into a pile of laundry in your basement," Brian insisted reasonably.

Jared blew his stack. "It's not in any pile of laundry! It just disappeared! It was a supernatural event of the unexplained!"

Leave it to Jared to add fuel to the fire when the joke was on him. Those Waterloo comedians howled.

The big thing at school that day was The Announcement. It was posted on the large bulletin board outside the office — the names of the players who had been chosen for the Waterloo Slapshot League All-Star team.

This wasn't just a great honor. It also meant you got to go to the tournament in Windsor to play against the select squads from fifteen other leagues.

A lot of people were gathered around the notice. Excited chatter filled the hallway, and high fives were flying in all directions. I'm kind of short, so I tried to rubberneck past the taller heads and shoulders in front of me.

"Make way for the press!" I called. It got me an elbow in the stomach and a lot of laughs. That's why I want to work for *Sports Illustrated.* No one takes the *Gazette* too seriously.

Alexia rolled her eyes. She stepped forward and plowed into the crowd like a harvester going through a wheat field. Trent and Josh waded through after her, and I slipped in between the two of them. When I looked up, there was the bulletin board.

The All-Star list was more or less what I expected. Half the kids were from the first-place Penguins, sponsored by Powerhouse Gas and Electric. I started to copy the roster into my reporter's notebook. King Diaper was on it, too, and a lot of other seventh-graders. I didn't recognize all the junior-high names. Trent was there, of course, and — my pencil point shattered. That was it for the Stars.

My reporter's sense tingled hard enough to electrocute me. This was a huge story. What an insult! I mean, we all liked Trent. But he was from Waterloo. This meant that not one single Marser had made the All-Star team. Okay, Josh had a lousy goals-against average. And I suppose Jared was better known as a joke than a winger. And our top defense pair looked pretty weird going down the ice, one forward, one backward. But what about Alexia?

She was a great two-way player, an awesome checker, and an accurate passer. She had even cracked the top twenty in scoring. Last week I interviewed a kid from the Flames. He told me their coach spent half a practice working on how to play against Alexia. She *belonged* on the All-Star team! It wasn't fair!

Josh put an arm around his sister's shoulders. "Sorry, Lex."

She didn't say anything, but I could tell she was upset.

"Well, what do you know!" announced Happer Feldman right in our faces. "There aren't any space hicks on the All-Star team!"

"No, here's one!" exclaimed Oliver Witt. "Some jerk named Trent Ruben. He ran off and joined the Martians, remember?"

Last season, when Trent was a Penguin, he and those two creeps were known as the HOT line — *H*apper, *O*liver, *T*rent. Now their center was a kid named Gavin, which made them the HOG line. Very fitting for pigs.

Happer turned his attention to Alexia. "Don't even bother looking for *your* name on there, *lady*," he sneered. "You think they're going to let a girl on the All-Star team?"

"Well, they should!" snapped Trent. "She's a better winger than either of you. This team is a joke if she's not on it!"

And Alexia did what I knew she was going to do because she's not like anybody else in the world. Instead of being mad at Happer and Oliver, she blew up at Trent.

In a quiet voice that carried up and down the hall, she said, "Who died and left you in charge of speaking up for me? Mind your own business!" And she stormed off, leaving Trent standing there with his mouth hanging open.

Oliver snickered. "Real classy team you're on now, Ruben."

Trent gave him a stony stare. "Like *you* would know anything about class."

We had to get out of there just to avoid a fight. I was still shaking my head as we walked away. "This is so wrong! There should be at least one Marser on the All-Stars."

Josh shrugged. "I guess our team started off so lousy — sure, we're better now. But our stars are nothing to brag about. You know — except for Lex."

"That's what I mean!" I persisted. "She should be on that list!"

Trent made a face. "Alexia could have more goals and assists than Wayne Gretzky and she wouldn't make that team. Not only is she a Marser, but she's also a girl. It's a double whammy."

"But don't you see how unfair that is?" I raved. "The All-Stars should be the best players, period! She's better than half those guys! King Diaper — big deal! She blows him away!"

"There's nothing we can do about it," Josh said sadly. "The league officials vote for the All-Star team. It's not up to us."

Okay, I thought. Maybe Josh was right. The team couldn't do anything. It wasn't a player's job to expose unfairness and fight for justice. That responsibility belonged to someone who could sift through the garbage and get to the truth; someone who could bring that truth to the public; someone like — a reporter.

At times like these, it stinks to be a kid. If I worked for ESPN, I could just go on TV and tell everybody about this big rip-off. At *Sports Illustrated*, I could do a whole cover story on it. But the *Waterloo Elementary School Gazette* was a once-a-month paper. By the time the next issue came out, the All-Star Tournament would be over!

I squared my shoulders and marched into Mrs. Spiro's class. "We need to publish a special emergency issue of the *Gazette*!"

She didn't even ask what for. She just said, "No."

"But —" I told her all that junk about the truth and the justice.

Mrs. Spiro, who was supposed to be a newspaperperson, gave me this long lecture about the cost of paper. Paper! What could be cheaper than that? Even B. B. Balls, the smallest and chintziest jawbreakers, cost a dime. You could get a whole lot of paper for that ten cents.

The bell rang. And for the next hour, I had to pretend to be thinking about English. But I had something much more important on my mind. I had to figure out a way to bring this outrage to everyone's attention.

But how?

‖‖‖‖ **Chapter 4**

Mars didn't have a fancy arena like the community center in Waterloo. Our rink was outdoors. The ice was kind of rough, which at first we thought was a minus. But practicing on it had made the Stars into fantastic skaters.

Anyway, we would have loved this pebbly rink even if it was prowled by man-eating timber wolves. It was the scene of the Stars' first-ever victory — against the Penguins, no less.

My father had said he'd try to make it to this practice. I was careful not to get my hopes up. You never know when a salesman's schedule is going to change. Dad was always running off to last-minute meetings and appointments. But when I rounded the corner to the rink, there he was. Not just there, but *on skates*, with a hockey stick, feeding practice passes to Jared, Cal, and Mike Mozak.

I raced over to the boards. "Hey, Dad!"

"Chipmunk! I've got a scoop for you! Your old father can still remember how to skate!"

He glided up to me and took a small package out of his pocket. "I brought you something. If you're going to make it to *Sports Illustrated*, you'll need this."

I got embarrassed. Dad must have picked up on my fake *Sports Illustrated* scrapbook cover. He sure didn't miss much.

I opened the parcel. I gawked. It was a palm-size tape recorder, the kind real reporters use! Perfect for interviews and for taping notes during exciting games.

I faced my dad. "There isn't anything you could have given me that would be better than this!"

He winked at me. "At your service."

I popped in the batteries. There was only one thing that could make this moment more perfect.

Dad must have read my mind. "Oh, incidentally —" He handed over a Volcano-Hot Cinnamon Lava-Ball. I had it tucked into my cheek so fast that I barely had time to take the paper off.

I hit *record* and began my first-ever taped interview.

24

"I'm speaking today with Mitch Adelman, father of the famous sportswriter Chipmunk Adelman. Oh — and here's Stars' coach Boom Boom Bolitsky." I hit the *stop* button. "Coach, I'd like you to meet my dad."

Dad said, "It's an honor to meet you, Boom Boom. I remember watching you in the NHL. Was it with the Red Wings or the Leafs?"

"Both," replied the coach.

As I mentioned before, Boom Boom hadn't exactly been a superstar as a pro. He got traded three times per season — that's when he wasn't being sent down to the minors. Not only was he a former Red Wing and Leaf; you had to add Flyer, Bruin, Black Hawk, Canuck, King, Penguin, and Ranger. The coach got around. If the NHL gave frequent-flyer miles, Boom Boom had earned himself a free trip to the moon.

Dad hefted his stick. "I hope you don't mind me crashing your practice."

Boom Boom grinned. "Crash away. We need all the help we can get." He cupped his hands to his mouth. "Okay, you guys! Gather around for the team thingamabob!"

I clicked on my tape recorder.

"Before we start with the whatsits —"

"Drills," I whispered into the condenser microphone.

"— does anybody have any doojigs or whatcha-macallits?"

"Questions or comments," I translated.

Jared put up his hand. Everybody groaned. Jared's comments were as notorious as they were bizarre.

"Coach, how come we never practice batting down the puck?"

Boom Boom looked surprised. "Practice it? You get your glove on the thingie, and you knock it down. There's nothing to practice."

"You don't understand," Jared insisted. "Last game I had to bat a puck down. And I did it wrong because we didn't practice how."

"And it hasn't come down yet," wisecracked Cal.

A few snickers escaped here and there. Even Boom Boom was holding back a chuckle. You could tell that he had no idea what to say.

"Well, Jared —" he began.

And who should step in to save the day? My dad.

"That's a very important point, Jared. I'd be happy to spend a little time doing, uh, batting-down drills with you." He added, "If it's all right with Coach Bolitsky."

Boom Boom looked relieved. "Fine, fine. Go ahead. Meanwhile we'll start our skating whatcha-macallits."

So the team practiced crossovers while my father

worked with Jared in the corner. I watched Dad lobbing pucks at Jared like he was tossing fish to the seals at the zoo.

Then Dad made the rounds of the team. He helped Josh learn to angle his blocker; he showed Brian and Mike some stickhandling tricks; he played defense against Trent on some one-on-ones; he even tried to explain to Cal why he was offside ninety percent of the time. That was a lost cause. Getting through to Cal was like trying to drill through titanium with a butter knife. But good old Dad was pretty sharp. He sized up Cal and decided to tell him a knock-knock joke. Not only that, but it was one that Cal had never heard before. Our winger hurled himself down right in the middle of the center face-off circle and howled with glee for a full five minutes.

When practice could finally begin again, Dad was right in the middle of the bodychecking drill. He made a big show of taking a spill every time anyone touched him. Laughter rang out in the cold late-afternoon air. Then Alexia came along and put Dad flat on his back for real.

I leaped the boards and rushed over. "Dad, are you okay?" I thought he was dead.

Groaning, he got back up on his skates again. He looked around and beckoned to the player who had decked him. "You — come over here."

Alexia glided up and pulled off her helmet. Long fair hair spilled out over her shoulder pads. She stared up at my father, her jaw stuck out defiantly.

I held my breath. I knew she was daring him to make a big deal about her being a girl.

But he never changed expression, never showed surprise, never even said, "Oh, wow, it's a girl!"

"Now *that's* a perfect shoulder check," he told the group. "Watch her, and do what she does, and you'll be just fine."

You could see Alexia's jaw relax. All the stiffness went out of her neck. She smiled at my father, and, believe me, Alexia doesn't smile that much.

I was thrilled. My dad was making a great impression on the Stars, and on Boom Boom, too. The coach seemed really happy to have another adult to help him run the practice.

Seriously, it was one of the greatest moments of my life. I had a jawbreaker in my cheek, a brand-new professional tape recorder in my hand, and I was reporting on my own dad, who was becoming a part of the story I was covering. It just didn't get any better than this! Dad even came with the team back to Mars Health Food for our after-practice meeting.

"I would like to propose a toast," he said, raising his glass of carrot juice, "to our All-Star, Trent. Good luck in the tournament."

For me, it was the first sour note — *clunk!* — in the beautiful symphony of my afternoon. Here I was, having fun, while this rotten league was getting away with shutting us Marsers out of the All-Star team.

Trent looked uncomfortable, too. "I don't know. Maybe I won't go."

Boom Boom was shocked. "What do you mean, you won't go? What kind of a negative thingamabob is that?"

"It's going to feel pretty weird playing with all those Penguins," Trent said unhappily. "Those guys have treated me like dirt since I've been a Star."

Alexia spoke up. "You'd better believe you're going," she declared, her reverse volume control almost down to zero. "Don't you dare wimp out because I didn't get picked. I don't want your charity!"

"You just need your teammates cheering you on," Mrs. Bolitsky told Trent. She turned to her husband. "Tell them, Boom Boom."

I could see the enthusiasm building up inside our coach. His praying-mantis eyes bugged out a little further. "I got this great whatsit," he began. "We'll all get into the gizmo and take a dingus to the hee-jazz —"

We were confused, but we weren't surprised. When Boom Boom's excitement level went up, his

English level went down. Now we were up to our elbows in doohickeys.

Mrs. B. bailed us out. "What Boom Boom means is that we're all going to Windsor to watch the championship game of the tournament."

"Oh!" gasped Cal. "What if my folks won't let me go?"

"Take it easy," laughed Boom Boom. "I've already phoned everybody's parents. They all said whatchamacallit."

"They all said yes," his wife translated. "We had to get permission because there's more. Windsor is right across the river from Detroit. And you know Boom Boom used to be a Red Wing. So he still has a few connections in the front office."

"We're all going to the Red Wings game on Saturday night," finished Boom Boom.

We got the dazzling supermodel smile from Mrs. B. "So bring your toothbrushes. We're staying over in a hotel."

The team went nuts.

"A real NHL game!" Josh breathed. "I can't believe it!"

"This is the greatest thing that's ever happened to me!" agreed Brian with reverence.

"We can see how Steve Yzerman himself bats the puck down!" exclaimed Jared.

I must have looked a little worried. After all, I wasn't a Star.

Boom Boom slapped me on the back. "Yeah, you too, Chipmunk. How could we go without our team whosis?"

"It sounds like the greatest trip in the world," moaned Trent. "And I have to miss it to play on a line with Happer stinking Feldman!"

Alexia laughed right in his face. "Look on the bright side, hotshot. We wouldn't be going if our wonderful teammate Trent hadn't made the All-Stars."

Kyle clutched at Boom Boom's sleeve. "You're not putting us on, right, Coach? This is definitely going to happen?"

Boom Boom grinned. "Cross my thingamabob. We just need one more volunteer with a big car."

"No, you don't!" My dad jumped up. "You're looking at your volunteer right here! I've got a rented van that'll seat six or seven kids."

My eyes must have bulged out like Boom Boom's. "Dad! Really? Gee, *thanks*!"

He smiled. "At your service."

Chapter 5 \ \ \ \ \ \

I dictated my latest headline idea into my tape recorder: *"Adelman Joins Stars Coaching Staff."*

No, not me. It was my father, right up there with Boom Boom behind the Stars' bench for their game against the Oriental Palace Panthers. I was thrilled. Boom Boom even let Dad deliver the pregame scouting report.

"I've been asking around about these Panthers," Dad told the team before the opening face-off. "Near as I can tell, they're not rough, but they're sneaky."

"Sneaky?" Jared repeated. "What do they do — put Krazy Glue in the referee's whistle? Hijack the Zamboni? Steal the puck?"

"No," guffawed Cal. "You're the only one who does that."

"Sneaky in hockey means doing thingamajigs when you know the ref isn't looking," Boom Boom explained.

"They're experts at not getting caught," Dad confirmed. "And if we do it back to them, *we'll* be the ones in the penalty box. So don't lose your cool."

The game started, and we knew right away that the scouting report was A-1 correct. I've never seen so much holding and hooking in my life.

The head sneak was a grade-seven kid named Luke Doucette. I mean, Trent won the opening face-off fair and square, but this creep reached down and held his stick. It was just for a second, and the referee missed it. But it was long enough for Luke to kick the puck to a Panther winger.

Pretty soon the Panthers were in total control. And every time the Stars would try to get something going, a little trip or a tiny bit of interference would stop the rush before it could even get to center ice. Then the Panthers' defense could just flip the puck back into the Stars' zone.

This went on until Jared decided to go after one of those high clearing passes. He hurled himself straight up like a high jumper. But he was so intent on getting at the puck that, instead of batting it, he caught it. It was such a spectacular athletic move that half of us clapped. It wasn't until the whistle blew that we remembered — closing your hand on the puck is a two-minute penalty.

"Great catch," jeered Luke as Jared took his seat in the penalty box. "Too bad this isn't baseball."

"I think we need more practice," Jared called to my father.

"Don't worry about it," Dad called back.

We should have worried, because the Panthers had a deadly power play. The four Stars formed a box to protect Josh. But nothing could stop Luke Doucette. He had an amazing wrist shot, even better than Trent's. It was the kind most kids don't develop until they're about sixteen. He could get the puck way up high anytime he wanted.

He parked himself in front of Josh and waited for his wingers to feed him. Pretty soon the right pass came along. With a flick of his wrists, Luke popped the puck over Josh's glove into the top corner of the net.

The Stars fought back. Trent wriggled away from two defenders who were draped all over him. He had to twirl around to break free. Facing the wrong way, he backhanded a perfect pass right onto the stick of a streaking Alexia. Her shot beat the goalie between his legs. Tie score.

The Mars fans cheered like crazy. I stood up and

held out my tape recorder to catch the roar of our support. Most teams had a few parents and brothers and sisters rooting them on. But a lot of Marsers always came to watch the Stars.

Boom Boom awarded Trent a humongous slap on the back. "Great whatchamacallit!" We all knew he meant "assist."

"Nice shot," Dad told Alexia. "Right in the five-hole."

So she wasn't good enough for the All-Stars? Yeah, right!

The goal was a big lift for Mars Health Food. But just before the end of the period, that rotten Luke got away with tripping Brian. He stole the puck, sailed out in front of Josh, and *pow*! He fired a snapper over Josh's blocker. Man, that shot was so perfectly aimed — right below the crossbar. Josh would have had to be Rubber Man to stop it.

It was 2–1 for the Panthers at the first intermission.

"They're *criminals*!" complained Brian, rubbing his leg where a stick had hooked him. "It's like playing against a gang of muggers!"

"And that Luke kid!" put in Alexia. "Cheap shots are an art form with him!"

"That's the kind of swell guy I have to play with on the All-Star team," Trent said sarcastically.

"Poor you," replied Alexia without much feeling.

"I'd rather have him on my team than play against him!" exclaimed Josh, with real fear in his eyes. "He's got a magic wand for a stick! He can shoot high as easy as flipping a coin!"

"We're only down by one dingus," Boom Boom reminded his team. "We can beat the Panthers if we don't sink to their whatchamacallit."

"Level," Dad interpreted.

I was impressed. You usually had to be with Boom Boom for weeks before you could start translating. I never knew my father was so smart!

The buzzer sounded to call the teams back for the second period.

It wasn't long before I was dictating a new headline into my tape recorder: "*Seesaw Battle.*"

Trent got a goal to tie the game at two. The Panthers took the lead again. Kyle got it back on one of his famous reverse rushes. The Panthers answered that one, too. And every single goal of theirs came from that kid Luke — always on a high wrist shot.

Okay, I'm biased. But the Stars were the better team here. The only reason the Panthers were winning was because of all that grabbing and holding they were getting away with. By this time, the things I was saying into my tape recorder were definitely not nice. Especially when we got a big scare. Late in the third period, that rotten Luke sleazed free for another monster wrist shot. Half an inch lower would have meant a sure goal. As it was, poor Josh smacked his head on the crossbar trying to get in front of it. Boom Boom had to use our time-out to get Josh over to the bench to make sure he was okay.

Our goalie was sweaty and exhausted. "I don't know how much more of this I can take, Coach! When he comes at me with that weird curvy stick —"

My dad jumped on that like a dog after a bone. "Curvy stick? How curvy?"

Trent, who took face-offs against Luke, made his best guess. "It's hard to say. Definitely curvier than mine."

Dad looked at Boom Boom. "What should we do, Coach?"

When Boom Boom thinks hard, his praying-mantis eyes whirl in his head. This time they were like pinwheels. Suddenly, he was standing atop the bench.

"*Ref!!*"

The man skated over. "Time's up, Stars."

Coach Bolitsky pointed at Luke Doucette. "Number whatsis is playing with an illegal doohickey! I want a thingamajig!"

Chapter 6 \\\\\\

The official stared at Boom Boom. "What?"

The team, Dad, and I all started translating at the same time. Out of the wild babble, the man was able to pull the words "number twelve," "illegal stick," and "measurement."

Silence fell as the timekeeper handed the ref the measuring box. If the stick really was illegal, then the blade wouldn't fit inside the opening. That would be a Panthers' penalty.

We all held our breath. If the stick turned out to be okay, it would be delay of game against the Stars. Trailing 4–3, the last thing we needed was to be shorthanded. Another Panthers' goal would put this game out of reach.

That rotten Luke tried to switch sticks with one of

his teammates. But the ref saw right through that. And it came as no surprise to anyone that the curve was too wide for the measuring slot. It was as illegal as a three-dollar bill.

The referee busted the blade with his skate so it could never be used again. Luke headed for the penalty box in a chorus of boos.

Boom Boom slapped my father on the shoulder. "Good call, Mitch."

I already knew what Dad was going to answer. "At your service."

It was the Stars' first man advantage of the game, and it was almost as if they'd been saving up. All those power plays they had truly deserved were wrapped up into these two minutes. They were awesome. They fired nine shots at the Panthers' goalie before Cal scored on a big-muscle wraparound from behind the net.

Tie score, 4–4.

From then on, the game was dizzying action. Both teams pulled out all the stops and fought hard for the go-ahead goal.

Luke had a couple of chances. But without his "special" stick, his wrist shot was flat and average. You could just see Josh gaining confidence as he stood up to the guy.

Enraged, Luke got even dirtier than before. He roared into the corner, hooking and tripping. And then he tried to get his stick around Alexia.

You may have figured out by now that Alexia doesn't like to be pushed around. After an entire game of cheap shots, she had finally devised a way to outsneak the sneaks. As the blade of Luke's stick came up into her chest, she imprisoned it with crossed arms. Then she twirled around, whipping Luke, who was hanging onto the butt end of his stick. With a terrified howl, Luke sailed in a half circle like he was attached to a helicopter rotor. And then she let go.

Wham! Luke Doucette hit the boards. I'm amazed he didn't go right through them.

"Last minute of play in the game," came the PA announcement.

Alexia passed off to Brian, who streaked up the ice. He was the fastest of all the Stars.

"Go, Brian!" I bellowed.

He approached the bench in the middle of a line change, just as Mike Mozak climbed over the boards. Now, I don't want to say Mike is slow. But you don't time him with a stopwatch; you use a calendar.

It was like the tortoise being rear-ended by the hare. Brian plowed into Mike from behind. And when the dust cleared, Brian was flat on his back, and the puck had somehow found its way onto Mike's stick.

Mike's skating style involved a lot of small choppy steps. So he always seemed to be moving like crazy when he was actually going nowhere at all. Six of his strides were equal to anybody else's one.

Since the Panthers were trying to defend against Brian, they broke their necks getting back to their own zone. So when Mike labored across the blue line, there was no checker anywhere near him. They were all crowded around the net.

Mike's shot was better than his skating, but it was also kind of unusual. We called it the "shovel shot." He pulled the puck way behind him. Then he unloaded with a long, sweeping motion, like a guy shoveling snow. With five defenders crowding the net, the goalie was completely screened. Even Mike couldn't see past all those sticks and skates to know that he had scored. But there was no mistaking the flash of the red goal light.

Final: 5–4, Stars.

The locker room was a blizzard of backslaps and high fives.

"I can't believe we won!" howled Josh. "They cheated, and we *still* beat them!"

"That stick measurement!" crowed Kyle. "I'll never forget it as long as I live."

Of course, Mike was at the center of a lot of congratulations. It was his first goal all year, and he couldn't have picked a better time for it.

"Listen to this, everybody!" I backed up my tape and hit *play*.

We heard "Aaaaaaaah — *Crunch!*"

"What was that?" asked Jared, mystified.

"That," I cackled, "is the sound of Luke Doucette flying into the boards."

The team made me play it six more times, and I had to promise to make Alexia her own copy.

Mrs. B. was handing out tofu granola squares and mango juice when Dad burst into the room, struggling with a big white box.

"Gather round, everybody," he called. And when we were all there, he threw open the lid. "Ta-*da!*"

We gawked. It was an enormous, beautiful, gooey, chocolatey cake! No, it was three cakes, each one a number:

5 0 0

"That's right!" shrieked Josh. "We're five and five now! We're playing five-hundred hockey!"

"Gee, thanks, Mr. Adelman!" breathed Jared.

"At your service."

Dad had all the trimmings — plastic forks, special paper plates with "Congratulations" written across them, and napkins to match.

The Stars fell on the offering like starving sharks. I really couldn't blame them. I mean, tofu versus cake? No contest.

I kind of felt bad for the Bolitskys. Gross as it was, their health food was a post-game tradition for the Stars. And here was Dad, upstaging them with delicious dessert. But the coach and his wife didn't seem upset at all. In fact, they each had a piece. So I didn't feel superguilty when I had three.

Trent was the only Star who stuck with his tofu granola square.

"Pssst," hissed Cal. "Are you crazy? You're eating tofu over chocolate?"

Trent shrugged. "You know, the taste is starting to grow on me."

I was amazed. "You *like* it?"

"Sure," he said. "Why not?"

I started counting reasons. I gave up at a billion.

Chapter 7

It kept eating away at me: No Marsers on the All-Star team. Every time I passed the bulletin board in front of the office, I did a slow burn.

I was so mad at the league. But I was mad at myself, too. It was my job as a reporter to fight this big rip-off. And what had I done so far? Nothing!

But what could I do? Mrs. Spiro wouldn't let me publish a special issue of the *Gazette*. She didn't want to waste *paper*! I almost spat at the bulletin board. Talk about wasted paper! There was a notice up for the Monopoly team and the kindergarten triangle band. The Nutrition Society had a two-pager, all about brussels sprouts! Every club, group, team, and association had flyers plastered all over the school.

Then it hit me. Mrs. Spiro said I couldn't publish a special *Gazette*. But she'd never said anything about making leaflets. I could print up a one-page notice demanding that Alexia be put on the All-Star team in the name of fairness. If I ran off eight, I'd have enough to tape one up in every hallway in the school. Hey, if the Barney the Dinosaur Fan Club deserved eight sheets of paper, then so did this! It would show those league officials as the stinkers they really were!

I ran across the hall and peered out the window to the parking lot. Perfect! Mrs. Spiro's rusty Subaru was just pulling out into the street. Most of the other teachers had already left.

I ran up to the *Gazette* office on the second floor. Jackpot — unlocked!

The room was a big storage area where the paper supplies were kept. There was also one computer, one printer, and the school's old Copymax machine. Not exactly *Sports Illustrated* but better than nothing.

I turned on the computer and sat down. I thought up a great headline and typed it in:

HOW CAN THEY SLEEP AT NIGHT?

The Waterloo Slapshot League has a lot of explaining to do.

The All-Star team is supposed to have the best players on it. So how come Alexia Colwin didn't get picked? Is it because she's from Mars? Or a girl? Or maybe both . . .

I dazzled the reader with statistics: goals, assists, plus-minus. I talked about her checking, her skating, and what a great captain she was. By the time I was done, an ape would have agreed that Alexia belonged on that team.

I also had a really great feeling in my heart — the feeling of the power of the press. The league wouldn't get away with this insult against Mars. I, Chipmunk Adelman, reporter, was making sure people found out about it.

I printed it up. It looked awesome, but there was something missing. In the newspaper business, a picture is worth a thousand words.

And I had one. It was the Stars' team photo, which had gone with my column in last month's *Gazette*. I rushed to the filing cabinet and dug it out. I ran it through the scanner and watched the image appear on my computer screen. There was Alexia, unsmiling, in the second row. I used the mouse to put a square around her face. Then I enlarged the picture so that it was a head-and-shoulders shot of the Stars' captain.

I heard the clang of the custodian's mop bucket. He'd made it to the second floor, which meant he'd be here in ten minutes. I had to work fast.

I printed the flyer with the picture on it. And if I do say so myself, it was a thing of beauty. I fit it into the Copymax machine and punched nine copies into the keypad — one extra for the big bulletin board in front of the office. Then I remembered. Our last *Gazette* came out kind of light and faded. The Copymax was low on toner.

Most photocopiers work on a toner cartridge that you click into the machine. This old clunker needed toner that you had to pour into a small container near the top. I picked up the toner bottle, unscrewed the cap, and started to fill the tank. And I found out why Mrs. Spiro doesn't let students do this job.

It's hard! Toner is fine black dust, and it has to be poured very slowly and gently. I had the custodian half a hall away. I had no time for this!

A puff of black powder wafted up into my face.

"A-choo!"

A sudden sneeze came out of my nose, and I dropped the bottle. And that's something you should never do.

The plastic jug bounced and skittered across the floor, spraying toner everywhere. And that stuff is so fine and so light that a thick black fog of it rose up in the room like a portable thundercloud.

Desperately, I dove for the bouncing bottle. But

just as I left my feet, I got another snootful of toner. I exploded into a series of violent sneezes in midair.

Wham! I plowed headfirst into the side of the Copymax. I'm not sure if I blacked out because everything was already black as the clouds of toner billowed around me.

Dazed, I hauled myself to my feet and stood there, gasping and snorting, holding onto the copies for dear life. I snatched up the bottle. Except for a few grains at the bottom, it was empty. I screwed the cap back on. I have no idea why.

I raced to the window and threw it open. What luck! It was a breezy day. Air currents swirled through the room, drawing some of the toner outside.

I looked down at myself. I was coal-black. I wouldn't be able to touch the flyers if I ever got them printed. I heard the janitor whistling. Oh, no! He was only two doors away! I had to get finished and get out of there!

I hit the start button and ran for the washroom across the hall. By the time I got cleaned up, my notices would be ready, and I could make a break for the stairs.

When I saw myself in the bathroom mirror, I almost dropped dead. Oh, sure, I knew I'd be dirty from all that toner. But I looked like Wile E. Coyote after his Road Runner bomb blew up in his face — wild-eyed, shaggy, and covered from head to toe with black stuff.

I soaped and I scrubbed. And, yeah, a lot of it came off. But my face and hands were stained and blotchy. The most I could do for my clothes was to try to sponge them off with a damp paper towel. At least it removed some of the caked-on black.

I opened the door a crack and peered out to make sure the coast was clear. Yikes! Mr. Sarkis was in the very next room! I tiptoed back into the *Gazette* office and silently shut the door behind me. The sight that met my eyes almost stopped my heart.

The Copymax machine was still working, churning out copy after copy. And as fast as my notices were coming out, they were blowing straight through the open window!

I staggered over to look outside. The air was white with them! Hundreds of them!

"But I only made nine copies!" I croaked out loud. I stared at the counting display. It was now printing number 416! That couldn't be right! Then I saw the keypad. I must have hit a couple of numbers by mistake when I was picking myself up off the floor. Instead of nine, it was set for 945!

Then there was a click. A split second later, the door was flung wide, and a horrified Mr. Sarkis was frozen there, looking at the wreckage inside.

"What the —?"

I admit it. I panicked. I threw my jacket over my head and ran past the custodian, into the hall, down the stairs, and out of the building.

As I headed for the bus stop, I could see my flyers still sailing out the window, one by one.

"Aw, come on, Mr. Sarkis! Pull the plug!" I cried.

I guess I shouldn't have been so hard on the poor guy. They probably didn't cover this in custodian school.

I caught a glimpse of myself in the glass of the bus shelter. No way could I go home like this. I mean, I looked like Pigpen from Charlie Brown comics.

I glanced behind me to see a trail of black footprints leading all the way from the school to the bus stop. Even if I could sneak into my house without Mom seeing me, I'd end up tracking toner all over the carpet. And how could I ever explain what happened to my clothes? This was a lose-lose situation!

Then it hit me. I had *two* parents in town these days!

I sprinted the half mile to the Waterloo Motor Inn. I tiptoed into the lobby, hoping no one would notice my disgusting, filthy self.

"Hold it right there, kid!"

Wouldn't you know it? The desk clerk was a sumo wrestler — or at least as big as one.

I just started babbling. "I'm here to see my father! He's a traveling salesman! He's only in town for a few weeks!"

"What is this stuff — mud?" It was now on the clerk's hands. "Geez, it doesn't come off!"

"Chipmunk?" My dad came walking in from the coffee shop. "What happened to you?" To the clerk he said, "It's okay. He's my son."

"What is he — a junior coal miner?"

"Yeah, Chipmunk," said Dad. "What have you been into?"

I was so used to dealing with Mom that I automatically launched into a lie.

"Uh — it's volcanic ash. You see, I'm doing a project on volcanoes —"

Then I remembered. This was *Dad*. He was just as flaky as I was. If anyone would understand, he would.

"Could we talk about it someplace more, you know, private?" I whispered.

"We'll go to my room," he agreed. "But take off your shoes. You're tracking that black stuff all over the floor."

We went upstairs, and I confessed. I mean, the

whole story, from the All-Star picks clear through to Mr. Sarkis busting in on me.

"I'm sorry to show up here like this," I finished. "But there's no way I could ever explain it to Mom. Not in a billion centuries!"

"Take it easy," he soothed. "No problem. Do I at least get to see this wonderful leaflet of yours?"

"I didn't even get one," I moaned. "They flew out the window. It was all for nothing!"

He laughed in my face, but at least he had a plan. "Okay, buddy. You jump in the shower, and I'll take your clothes to the hotel Laundromat. When you get out, phone Mom and say I picked you up after school, and you're staying with me for dinner. Got it?"

I could have hugged him, but he was wearing a really nice suit, and he didn't deserve a hug from me.

"Thanks, Dad!"

"At your service."

| | | | | | ___Chapter 8___

It took forty minutes in the shower to get all that toner off me. While I was on the phone with Mom, I checked myself over in the mirror. I looked human again, except that I was getting a bruise on my forehead. Well, that was easy to explain. I bonked my head. It was totally true. I practically put my cranium through the side of the Copymax machine. I was lucky to be alive!

The door swung open. "Anybody looking for a pile of clothes?"

Dad had even washed my sneakers. I got dressed, and we went out to dinner. We were just crossing the parking lot when *whap*! A piece of wind-tossed paper smacked me right in the face. I was about to brush it away when I saw the words *HOW CAN THEY SLEEP AT NIGHT?*

"It's my flyer!" I exclaimed, horrified. "How did it get all the way over here from school?"

My father shrugged. "It's windy."

That's when I noticed a lot of other papers blowing around in the breeze. Across the street, a lady had managed to snare one and was reading it.

"I'm dead!" I moaned.

Dad laughed. "What are you complaining about? You did it to get some attention."

I shivered. I had a sinking feeling that I was going to get more attention than I bargained for.

I considered faking sick the next morning, but decided I'd better not. It would look too suspicious if I was the only guy absent the day after someone trashed the *Gazette* office and littered Waterloo with four hundred sheets of paper.

So I was up bright and early, flossing and brushing — eleven cavities, remember? Downstairs, my mom was singing her usual tune:

"Hurry up, Clarence! You're going to miss the bus!"

I looked into the mirror and almost swallowed my toothbrush. The bruise on my forehead was now in full bloom. But that wasn't the bad part. When I fell yesterday, I must have whacked my head against the raised metal logo on the copier. Because this bruise spelled out in red, purple, and blue: Copymax.

I guess I howled because Mom rushed to the foot of the stairs. "Is everything okay, dear?"

"Yeah, Mom." Oh, sure. Peachy. Except that this bruise was like wearing a sign that said: *Here he is. The guy who did it all. Arrest him. Kill him. He deserves it.*

Then I spotted Mom's makeup on the top shelf. Saved! I slopped it on over my bruise like Wite-Out on a typing mistake. And it worked! I mean, it looked a little lumpy and still kind of bruised. But at least it didn't say Copymax anymore.

Mom never knew the difference as I breezed through the kitchen and headed out the door.

I stopped dead on the front walk. There in our flower bed was a copy of my flyer. Another was nestled in the next-door neighbor's tree. I couldn't believe it. These papers had made it the two miles to Mars!

On the school bus, every single kid had seen the notice. No one could talk about anything else.

"'How can they sleep at night?'" Jared chortled with glee. "This is so great!"

"It really says it all," agreed Brian. "I wonder who did it?"

"Who do you think?" snarled Alexia in reverse volume control. "Trent Ruben, that's who. *He's* the one who won't shut up about me not being picked for the All-Stars. When I get my hands on that big-mouth, I'm going to send him on a permanent vacation away from his teeth!"

I shuddered and sank a little lower in my seat.

Josh rolled his eyes at his twin sister. "Can't you learn to take a compliment for once in your life? *Somebody* — we don't know who — is trying to stick up for you! Trying to stick up for all of us! What's making you so mad?"

Alexia slapped her flyer in disgust. "Nobody fights my battles, least of all a clown like Trent Ruben! It's the stupidest thing I've ever seen! It's not even my picture!"

"*Huh?*" I joined the crowd peering over Alexia's shoulder. She was right! It was so blurry because the photograph had been so enlarged that you couldn't really tell the difference. I guess I zeroed in on the wrong face or something.

"It's Cal!" I blurted.

"Really?" said Cal. "Hey, yeah! Cool! I'm in a flyer!"

"As a girl," added Jared.

"Shut up."

"Everybody sit down," came Mrs. Kolodny's

voice from the front. "We're about to enter the earth's gravitational field."

"You know," mused Kyle as we took our seats, "there's no way Trent did this. How could a kid send millions of papers all over the place in just one night? I'll bet they were dropped out of a helicopter! It had to be an adult."

"Maybe it was Boom Boom," suggested Brian. "He knows what a big rip-off it is that Lex didn't make the team."

"No way," said Alexia. "This whole thing is in English. If the coach wrote it, it would be full of thingamajigs and doohickeys."

"Mrs. Bolitsky speaks English," Cal reminded everybody.

Jared snapped his fingers. "I'll bet it was Mr. Adelman! He loves our team! And you know he's the kind of guy who makes stuff happen. Look at the way he's getting us names for the backs of our jerseys."

In all the excitement, I'd almost forgotten. Dad was arranging with some guy he knew to get player names for the Stars to sew on their hockey sweaters. As a major team booster, he looked like the prime suspect. I had to clear this up.

"It wasn't my dad," I said carefully. "I was with him last night. If he was planning something big, I would have been able to tell."

"Well, then, who did it?" wondered Josh. "I want to meet him and shake his hand."

"You can't shake hands with someone who's got two broken arms," Alexia promised in a low voice.

As the bus pulled into our parking space in front of the school, we could see Trent. He was waiting there, holding up a flyer and grinning.

"Have you guys seen this?" he asked excitedly as we all piled off the bus. "Who did it?"

Alexia skewered him with a lancelike stare. "Very smooth, hotshot. You just keep on pretending that you're not the lowest dirtbag in Waterloo."

Poor Trent's mouth hung open in shock. She crumpled up the flyer and jammed it inside. Then she stormed into the building.

Trent just stood there with his mouth full of paper. "Wha' di' I do thi' 'ime?" he mumbled.

The school was a madhouse. It seemed like every kid had brought in a flyer or two. And they talked about plenty more out there, blowing all over the place. I must have heard a dozen stories about how each person picked up a copy — out of a tree, out of a fence, out of the air, on the grill of a car, out of a dog's mouth; you name it.

The nine o'clock announcements were scary. Mr.

Lambert, the principal, got on the PA and demanded that the guilty party come forward. In English, Mrs. Spiro raved about the wasted paper and a ninety-five-dollar bottle of toner. In the cafeteria, Mr. Sarkis harangued us about a mess that had taken him four hours to clean up.

"All that spilled toner!" he ranted. "It flies like dust, but it's worse than India ink! It gets all over the place!"

Yeah. Tell me about it.

It was another rough day to be a Marser, but not as rough as I expected. For every Waterloo jerk who was really steamed, there was also one who thought maybe we had a point. A lot of girls wondered if Alexia had been kept off the All-Star team just for being female.

Then there was Happer Feldman. "I told you we never should have let those Martians in our league!" he declared in gym class that afternoon. "They've been nothing but trouble ever since —"

Wham!

That dummy should have known to keep his big mouth shut during a dodgeball game. Especially when Alexia was playing.

"Hey, Chipmunk," called Jared. "What's that on your forehead?"

My forehead?! I yelled, "Bathroom break!" and ran for the lockers. I caught sight of myself in the mirror and gasped, "Oh, no!"

All that sweating from dodgeball had washed the makeup right off my face. My bruise was there again, in living color: Copymax.

This was a major disaster! If any of the teachers saw my head and put two and two together, my goose was cooked. I had to cover this bruise. But Mom's makeup was in our bathroom, two miles away!

I looked around, mind racing. If I took off my underwear and wrapped it around my head, would anyone notice it wasn't a bandanna? Suddenly, my eyes fell on the Lost and Found box. I dove for it. Socks, shoelaces, a bran muffin — what kind of an idiot brings a bran muffin to gym class? Ah — jackpot!

I pulled out a small sweatband and slipped it around my head. It squeezed like a python. And it was bright pink, with a palm tree on the front. But at least it didn't say Copymax.

"Everything okay, Clarence?" asked Mr. Vanderhoof when I returned to the gym.

"Oh, fine. I just had to get my sweatband."

Jared stared at me. "That was *yours*? It's been in the box for two years!"

"I've been busy!" I snapped. Being a reporter is a high-stress job.

Chapter 9

"The litter!" Mom said as we rattled over the bridge into Waterloo. "Hundreds of flyers blowing all over the county. They've been seen as far away as Woodstock! Mrs. Colwin says Alexia thinks it was the Ruben boy."

"It definitely wasn't Trent," I assured her.

"What makes you so sure?"

"I'm the team reporter," I said. "Reporters know stuff."

She shot me a sharp sideways look. "You know who did it?"

There were two possible answers: the truth, and the one I used. "No."

"Sorry, dear." Mom shrugged her apology. "I have to confess that I suspected you might be mixed up in it somehow. You know, with that headband you wear. I thought maybe the pink might mean you support girls on the All-Star team."

"Don't you know anything about style?" I told her, highly insulted. "This headband is the latest fashion! The whole school's wearing them!" In fact, the only reason I was still suffering in that supertight torture device was because I couldn't find a baseball hat that came down low enough to cover my Copymax bruise.

We parked and walked in the door marked WEL-COME TO PARENT-TEACHER NIGHT. The hallways were packed with students and their mothers and fathers. Not one single kid had on a pink headband with a palm tree on it.

Kyle waved at us through the crush of people. "Hi, Chipmunk! Still wearing the pink thing, huh?"

Mom shot me a suspicious look. "Latest fashion?"

Caught again. "You want me to be an independent thinker, don't you?"

"I'd settle for any kind of thinker." She consulted her watch. "We're late, Clarence. Let's hope Mrs. Spiro hasn't started with another parent already."

She clicked down the hall on her high heels. Mom took school stuff pretty seriously. I had to scramble to catch up with her outside Mrs. Spiro's room.

We both saw it at the same time. Yes, my teacher

had another parent in there, all right. But the other parent was *Dad*!

He must have told a joke because Mrs. Spiro was laughing like crazy. Dad has a lot of great jokes. It's a salesman thing. Let me tell you, he must have knocked off a rocket-powered rib-tickler to get *Mrs. Spiro* to giggle. She has no sense of humor at all!

Dad spotted me. "Hey, Chipmunk, we were just talking about you!" Spying Mom's disapproving eyes he added, "I mean, Clarence."

"Hi, Dad!"

"How has Clarence's work been?" Mom asked Mrs. Spiro.

"Top of the heap," Dad jumped in. "Now why don't the three of us see if we can track down the nearest pizza — my treat."

"Let's get finished here first," my mother insisted. She turned to Mrs. Spiro. "Clarence is devoting months and months of English class to being a 'team reporter.' I'd like to hear why this is a good idea from somebody besides him."

Mrs. Spiro smiled. "Don't worry, Mrs. Adelman. When Clarence is writing about the Stars, he does better work and more of it. I just wish he would stay on topic instead of spending so much time talking about jawbreakers."

"That problem is *over*," Mom informed Mrs. Spiro. The glare she shot me was at least radioactive. Like you could get a cavity from just writing the word.

Dad tried to bail me out by changing the subject. "Hey, buddy, which seat is yours? That one?"

It wasn't hard to spot. I had stenciled the *Sports Illustrated* logo onto the desktop in washable Magic Marker.

"Dad — no!" I hissed.

You see, my desk is a junk heap, packed in under extreme pressure. My father tried to pull out a textbook. It was stuck, so he gave a bit of a yank.

The entire contents of my desk exploded into his lap — crumpled papers, mangled notebooks, a plastic boomerang, an old sweat sock, a container of dental floss (unopened), and — gasp! — the Guavaberry Mouth Mangler I'd gotten from Dad after dinner on the day of the *Gazette* office disaster.

Running full speed, I caught it on the first bounce and hid it in my shirt pocket. That purple ball was in plain view for a second and a half, tops! But my mom — she was born with jawbreaker radar. Not only did she recognize a Mouth Mangler through a blizzard of flying junk; she also figured out exactly who gave it to me.

She glowered. "Aw, Mitch. Why do you keep feeding him candy?"

Dad wasn't saying "At your service" now. In fact, he didn't open his mouth at all.

I instantly knew two things: First, I would never get even a lick of that Mouth Mangler. And second, pizza with my parents tonight was definitely off.

I expected to get one of Mom's famous lectures. Instead, we made the two-mile drive back to Mars in complete silence. It was twice as bad as getting chewed out.

Finally, just as we were going into the house, I couldn't hold back. "Dad didn't give me that Mouth Mangler. It was — like — a free sample!"

"From the Jawbreaker-of-the-Month Club?" she asked sarcastically.

A bad liar shouldn't ever get too fancy.

Then Mom did something I didn't expect. She smiled.

"Remember the time when you were ten and Dad promised to take you fly-fishing?"

I nodded. I remembered, all right. How could I forget?

"He bought you everything," Mom went on. "The best rod and reel, a tackle box — even a floppy hat with lures on it. And remember? You got up at four in the morning and stood on the front porch in those hip waders that were bigger than you —"

"And he didn't come," I finished bleakly. "I waited till lunchtime."

"I'm not trying to say your father's a bad person," she continued. "We both know that's not true. But people who depend on him too much usually end up disappointed. You know?"

I flopped down on the couch. "Get real, Mom. I'm not ten years old anymore."

"No, you're eleven."

"Almost twelve," I insisted. "What I'm trying to say is I know all about Dad. It was me who got left with a half-finished go-cart for the big race; me who flew my own kite in the father-and-son contest. When you spend eight hours in rubber hip waders in the middle of an August heat wave, you learn a thing or two — I mean, besides how to get athlete's foot."

Mom laughed. "You're eleven, all right. Going on thirty."

"I know that Dad's only here on business," I went on. "And one of these days, business is going to take him someplace else. But that doesn't mean I can't enjoy it while he's around."

"Of course you should enjoy his company," my mother agreed. "He's a terrific guy. This is just a little, you know, reality check. I don't want to see you disappointed again."

"I'm cool," I promised. "You should see the way the team loves Dad! Jared practically wants to adopt him! He's a huge help to Coach Bolitsky! And he's going on the Windsor trip with us!"

Mom looked worried. "Maybe the reality check should be passed on to the Stars."

"Are you kidding?" I cried. "Dad's even going to get everybody's names to sew on the back of the team jerseys! He's got it all set up with a guy he knows."

"Your father always 'knows a guy,'" Mom said quietly.

"Not even the *Penguins* have their names on their shirts!" I insisted.

"Remember —" she warned. "You and I know Dad. The team doesn't."

I was kind of mad at her. What did she expect me to do — go to the Stars and bad-mouth my own father? Besides, how did she know that Dad hadn't changed — just a little? Maybe she was jealous that he was all about fun and hockey and awesome trips, and she was all about dentists and report cards and flushing perfectly good jawbreakers down the toilet! Dad was practically a Star by now. And if there was one thing I learned from the first day Mars got a team, it was that loyalty was everything.

I did my homework up in my room that night, being loyal to my teammate, Dad.

But just before I went to bed, a thought that had been nagging at me for several days broke through. The giant "500" cake that Dad had bought to celebrate the Stars victory over the Panthers — what a great thing to do! Only — he had to order that cake *before* the game. What if we'd lost? The team record wouldn't have reached .500, and that cake would have ended up in the garbage. Three cakes, really. Custom-baked. It must have been fifty bucks worth of dessert.

I shook myself angrily. What was I worrying about? We *did* win. And the cake was a fantastic, generous, perfect gift from a proud parent. And yet —

Forget it. Too much thinking. I climbed into bed and switched on my clock radio.

"If those statistics are true," the announcer was saying, "then she *belongs* on the All-Star team."

I sat bolt upright. All-Star team? *She?*

"We should have kept the league Waterloo-only," complained some guy on the phone. "It would have saved us a lot of aggravation — and a big garbage cleanup. We're talking hundreds of flyers. They should arrest whoever's responsible."

"Fair is fair," insisted another man. "I didn't want

the Martians, either. But now that they're in, we have to give them equal consideration for the All-Stars. Even for a girl."

Wait a minute! This was *SportsLine*, an *adult* show! All these callers were grown-ups! They were usually talking about Wayne Gretzky and Jerry Rice, not Alexia Colwin and the Waterloo Slapshot League All-Stars! What was going on?

The answer put a lump in my throat the size of a golden retriever. My accident in the *Gazette* office had sent so many flyers all over the place that the whole county had seen them.

"Whoever did this is right," insisted a new caller, a woman. "How *can* they sleep at night?"

Oh, man, was I in trouble! I switched off the radio with a shaky hand. But I couldn't help feeling just a little bit proud. I mean, talk about mission accomplished. Alexia got cheated and now everybody knew — thanks to Chipmunk Adelman.

And the power of the press.

Chapter 10 \\ \\ \\ \\ \\

By the Stars' next game on Saturday, the bruise on my forehead hadn't even begun to fade. Copymax: I was a human billboard for the company. I had to wear that stupid pink headband every minute of every day, even while sleeping. The last thing I needed was for Mom to wander into my room in the middle of the night and see it.

I couldn't even change headbands. Not after blabbing to Mom about how high-fashion the pink one was. Anyway, it squeezed like a vice grip, but at least I didn't have to worry about it falling off. One slipup was all it would take to sink me. This All-Star kerfuffle was turning into the biggest news in town!

One at a time, every Marser plus Trent got called to the office so Mr. Lambert could ask us if we knew who did it. The Waterloo newspaper had an article on it every single day. They had comments from players, their parents, league officials, even the mayor. He mostly talked about how expensive it was to clean up four hundred sheets of paper.

The only person who had absolutely nothing to say on the subject was Alexia herself — either that or her reverse volume control was cranked down so low that no one could hear her. She refused to be interviewed by the paper. And when I turned on my tape recorder in the back of the Mars Health Food truck on the way to the game, she snatched it right out of my hands. Before my horrified eyes she popped out the batteries and dropped them in a tub of organic pickles.

"Hey!" I dove for the plastic barrel. But just as I got the top off, Boom Boom wheeled around a sharp corner. A tidal wave of pickle water erupted out of the container and sprayed all over the players. I was lucky the whole tub didn't tip over.

"Come on, Chipmunk!" snapped Kyle, mopping greenish brine off the rearview mirror on his helmet.

"Pee-yoo! This stuff stinks!" added Jared.

"It's not my fault!" I fished out my batteries and slammed the lid back down. I looked daggers at Alexia. "Freedom of the press!" I shouted at her.

It's impossible to get the best of Alexia, especially when she's in a bad mood. "The press is free to mind its own business," she said quietly.

Trent was waiting for us at the community center. "You guys have got to see this!" he exclaimed.

He led us into the building and down the hall to the small room that served as the league office. We peeked in the half-open door. There at the desk sat Mr. Feldman, the president, Happer's uncle. (Family resemblance: They were both jerks.) He was struggling to go through a *mountain* of mail.

"I don't understand," Cal said with a frown. "Why would a mean guy like Mr. Feldman get so many letters?"

"This is because of the flyer!" Josh's excitement level rose as he caught on. "People are writing in to support Lex for the All-Star team!"

Trent nodded. "And that many letters couldn't all come from Mars. A lot of them must be Waterloo people complaining that it isn't fair."

Alexia cast Trent a withering glare. "You just can't seem to shut up about your precious flyers, can you?"

"They aren't *my* flyers," Trent retorted. "But whoever made them is a genius. Now the whole town sees how you got ripped off."

"Yeah?" she challenged, her voice dropping fast. "How do you know those letters don't say 'Bravo, Mr. Feldman! We don't want any Martian girls contaminating the great Trent Ruben and his All-Star team'?"

"I don't think so, Lex," put in Josh. "Mr. Feldman looks pretty upset. That probably means a lot of people are on your side."

Well, *that* turned out to be true. We found out for sure when the Stars came out of the locker room for their warm-up. As soon as Alexia stepped onto the ice, a high-pitched cheer went up in the arena, followed by a chant of *"All-Star! . . . All-Star! . . . All-Star! . . ."*

I fumbled with my recorder to get it on tape. It was amazing! The stands were jam-packed. I mean, sure, the Stars always got pretty good turnouts, but these weren't all Marsers. It looked like every elementary-school girl in the county was here. Someone had made up signs because they were waving all over the place. These showed the silhouette of a woman — the kind you see on a ladies' bathroom — inside a big star.

Boom Boom was bewildered. "Where did all these whosises come from? And why do they have thingamabobs?"

Dad took one look at the signs and broke into a broad grin. "Don't you get it? Girls can be All-Stars! They're supporting Lex!"

He flashed me a knowing wink. It was kind of cool sharing the secret with my dad, just the two of us. You wouldn't believe how loud he laughed the first time I showed him the Copymax bruise. It was almost enough to make me forget how much trouble I was in.

I expected things to calm down once the game started. Instead, just the opposite happened. Every time Alexia touched the puck, all those girls went nuts. If there was a hole in the middle of the ice, I think she would have crawled inside it.

Our opponents were the Hilltop Roto-Rooter Avalanche. They were a pretty lousy team except for their goalie, Lennox Kerr, who was the netminder for the All-Stars. They weren't used to playing in front of so many people, and the rambunctious crowd got them all riled up. Pretty soon, some junior-high kid took a run at Alexia, cross-checking her into the boards.

Dad and Boom Boom shouted for a penalty, but they were drowned out by the howls from Alexia's new fans. Up went the referee's arm, and the offender skated over to the penalty box. I think he was grateful to be there. If the ref had sent him into the stands, those girls would have torn him to pieces.

"Whatchama-doojig!" bellowed Coach Bolitsky.

"Power play!" translated Dad.

I leaned excitedly over the bench. Improving the power play was one of the areas that the coach had put my father in charge of. It was easy to see the results. Trent won the face-off and passed to Alexia, who took a booming slapshot.

"Sure goal!" I yelled into my tape recorder.

Out of nowhere came Lennox Kerr. He went into a split, kicking the puck into the corner. Cal dug it out, and fed Kyle at the point. Our defenseman faked a shot, then sliced in on goal on a backwards rush. Just before the slot, Kyle dished the puck to Trent, who sizzled a low backhand on net.

"He scores —" I began.

But Lennox stopped that one, too. The Stars' forwards hacked at the rebound. Lennox made — I counted — *five* more saves before smothering the puck.

Boom Boom and Dad exchanged pained looks.

"Hot whosis," said the coach.

"Hot goalie," my father agreed.

The Stars' power play unit skated rings around the hapless Avalanche. But somehow Lennox got himself in front of every shot. He even stopped one of Trent's classic dekes. By the end of the first period, the shots-on-goal counter said 19–3 in favor of the Stars. But the score was still 0–0.

"Too bad we don't have those names for the back of our jerseys yet," Jared told my dad in the locker room. "We could really use them out there today!"

I stared at him. "What difference would *that* make?"

Jared shrugged. "We'd look so cool that the other team would get, you know, demoralized. Then they'd play worse."

Coach Bolitsky had more practical advice — sort of. "When you run into a hot whosis, don't lose your whatsit. Just keep shooting the gizmo. Eventually, he'll make a thingamajig."

"Mistake," translated Dad.

Josh pulled off his mask and turned to his sister. "How about all that support you're getting, Lex? What do you think of those flyers now?"

Alexia silenced him with a look that would have stopped a clock.

In the second period, I dictated my headline idea into my tape recorder. It was a one-worder: *"Frustration!"*

The Stars were dominating the Avalanche — out-skating them, outchecking them, and outshooting them. But Lennox Kerr was unbeatable in net.

"It's like trying to score on Dominik Hasek!" complained Cal after the All-Star goalie had robbed him with a flailing blocker.

"Or a brick wall," added Alexia.

"Don't get crazy," Dad soothed.

But crazy was exactly the word for the way the Stars were playing. Shut out cold by Lennox, they were trying *too* hard to make something happen. And it was starting to get them in trouble.

Speedy Brian went on an end-to-end rush that was so fast he couldn't stop himself. He dug his blades into the ice, but the rest of him kept on going. He tumbled head over heels to land in a heap in the corner. Cal launched himself after a rebound, tripped, and smashed his helmet into the goalpost. Jared was wired, trying to bat down every puck that was more than six inches above the rink. He looked like he was playing handball, not hockey. Kyle was breathing so hard that he fogged up his rearview mirror, so he couldn't see where he was going anymore. He took some earthquake-force checks from the Avalanche defensemen. One time he reversed straight into the Zamboni gate, flipped over the boards, and landed in the pile of wet snow beside the big machine.

Even Trent was taking wild shots. Half of them bounced harmlessly off Lennox's body. The rest the goalie either gloved or handled with a lightning stick. *Nothing* got behind him!

Well, almost nothing. In the third period, Jared took a wild leap to bat down a high backhand just inside the face-off circle. His flailing glove hammer-fisted the puck over Lennox's shoulder and into the net. The red goal light flashed on, and the crowd erupted in deafening cheers.

Chapter 11

The referee waved his arms. "No goal!" he ruled. "You can't score on a hand pass!"

"Aw, come on!" Jared groaned. "What a stupid rule! How did a great sport like hockey get such a stupid rule?"

Cal gave him a playful elbow. "Maybe it was another supernatural event of the unexplained — like when that puck disappeared down your neck."

Jared flushed red. "Quit making fun of me! That was a real thing!"

I guess those Alexia fans didn't know hockey rules much better than Jared. Somehow they got the idea that the goal was disallowed because the officials were biased against the Stars for having a girl on the team. Boos rang out in the community center. Then they started stomping on the metal bleachers. It created a thunderlike crashing so loud that Mr. Feldman came out of his office to investigate the noise.

Coach Bolitsky called a time-out to get his team under control. But he was more agitated than any of the players. His bald crown glistened with perspiration, and his bulging eyes beamed like car headlights. He tried to give a pep talk, but it came out all doohickeys.

My father had to take over. "Calm down, you guys," he ordered. "You're acting like we're down ten goals. It's *nothing-nothing*. We're not even losing."

Then everything fell apart. The Avalanche iced the puck, but Kyle didn't see it in his foggy mirror. The winger beat him to it and centered it in front of the net. Alexia leveled her man with a shoulder check, but the pass hit her skate and dribbled back out to the defenseman at the point.

Pow! Okay, it wasn't much of a shot — low, and not very hard. But it hit the fallen center in the face mask and deflected past Josh into the net. My heart lurched. The Avalanche had finally broken the scoreless tie.

Mars Health Food fought back, blasting away at the superstar goalie. Rush after rush led to great scoring opportunities. The shots-on-goal counter read 43–9 in favor of the Stars. But the only scoreboard that mattered said 1–0, Avalanche.

The Marsers roared with excitement. But all those Alexia supporters were getting kind of restless. I mean, she was playing a strong game. But it takes a die-hard hockey fan to appreciate checking, passing, and defense. Those girls had come to see Alexia score ten goals and blow everybody away.

They did what bored people do: They fidgeted; they put down their signs; they talked. It was no big deal. But some of the boys in the crowd tried to rub it in Alexia's face.

"Hey, girlie!" came a shout from the stands. "What happened to your cheering section?"

"Your fan club's turning into a Tupperware party!" came another.

Some jerk called out, "No girls on the All-Star team!" and that led to a chant. "No girls! . . . No girls! . . . No girls!"

"Shut up!" Trent bellowed at the bleachers.

Cal reached out to make a poke-check. But at that moment, Alexia drove her shoulder into the same Avalanche player from behind. The hit was so hard that the winger *and* Cal went flying. Alexia picked up the puck and started down the ice.

Picture a charging rhino on skates; that was

Alexia's rush. She didn't make a single deke. She didn't even try to stay away from the defensemen. She just went straight forward, full speed ahead. Anybody who tried to stop her got flattened.

Trent swooped out in front of her. It was a play they'd practiced a hundred times — crossing paths to confuse the goalie; quick pass; quick shot. But Alexia was so focused on the net that she didn't even see him. Trent had to dive out of the way to avoid being steamrollered.

Lennox came out to cut down the angle. But instead of shooting, Alexia sped up. Even through his wire mask, I could see Lennox's eyes widen in horror as he realized that she was going to squash *him*, too.

He scrambled to back up, but he stumbled. And as he reeled to right himself, she slipped the puck between his pads into the net.

All those girls exploded to their feet, hurling their signs high in the air. One minute a cloud of placards was suspended above the rink. Then the entire ice surface was carpeted with the stuff. Players began to slip, slide, and fall as their skates hit cardboard.

"All Star! . . . All-Star! . . ." The chant was back again, but a lot of boys were still shouting, "No girls! . . . No girls! . . ."

I honestly wondered if my next article would be about a hockey game or a riot.

"Qui-et!!!"

It was Mr. Feldman, standing red-faced at center ice, shouting into the league's electric megaphone. Silence fell.

"This game is officially over," the president declared. "The Stars forfeit. The Avalanche wins."

"Forfeit?!" bellowed Coach Bolitsky. "Why?"

"League rules," Mr. Feldman's amplified voice echoed throughout the arena. "Each team is responsible for controlling its own fans."

"They're not our fans!" I babbled. "They're total strangers! Just a bunch of people off the street!"

The Avalanche players celebrated like crazy. They tried to skate a victory lap and wound up scattered like tenpins over the littered signs. But at least they *won*.

That rotten Mr. Feldman even ruled that the Stars had to stay behind and clean up the rink. I thought Boom Boom would give him an argument. But the coach seemed more concerned with getting his angry players calmed down. I was shaking with rage myself. This was my fault! My flyers had brought those girls here today!

Dad read my mind. "Take it easy, buddy. You can't blame yourself."

"But we're not five hundred anymore!" I cried. "After the cake and everything!"

"Tomorrow is another day," he soothed.

The girls booed for a while. But eventually, when they realized they couldn't change anything, they just went home.

Lennox Kerr stopped in front of Alexia. "They're right, you know," he offered shyly. "You should have made the All-Stars." And he zigzagged out the gate, using the scattered cardboards as stepping-stones.

I know for a fact that Mr. Feldman heard the whole thing. He was standing *right there*! But he pretended to be looking up at a broken light on the scoreboard.

He also ignored my new headline idea — even though I recorded it right in his ear: *Another Big Rip-Off Against Mars!*

▌▐▐▐▐ _Chapter 12_

The Wednesday before the All-Star Tournament was Spirit Day at Waterloo Elementary School. It was an annual event. Everybody wore athletic uniforms, crests, and hats. It was a rah-rah, support-your-team type of thing. And even though we were still smarting from the forfeit last weekend, we Marsers were pretty psyched. Sure, we'd played Waterloo sports before. But around here, there was no bigger deal than the Slapshot League. Finally, we had our own hockey team to cheer about.

The school halls were a carnival of color. Club logos blazoned everywhere. Pennants and stickers were displayed on lockers. Even the teachers got in on it. Mrs. Spiro squeezed into her high-school cheerleading outfit, pom-poms and all. Mr. Lambert dressed up as Shaquille O'Neal — only short, fat, and with a bushy red beard. Mr. McGinnis, who came from Scotland, used to play this weird sport where you throw something like a telephone pole — no lie! Anyway, the funny part is he came to school in a kilt that violated the short-skirt rule by at least three inches. But he didn't get in trouble. Anything goes on Spirit Day.

Since it was hockey season, Waterloo Slapshot League jerseys were the most popular outfits. I got Coach Bolitsky to lend me an extra Stars sweater. The green kind of clashed with my headband, but then again, it was hard to find any boys' clothes that went with bright pink.

All the league teams were well represented. Led by Happer and Oliver, the Penguins were the loudest and most obnoxious of them all. Big surprise.

"Look at them," sneered Alexia. "They think they own the world."

"They do," I reminded her. "They're undefeated, except for the time we beat them — and that was kind of a fluke. I didn't think they'd be so good without Trent."

"Where *is* Trent?" asked Josh.

We all spotted him at the same time, in front of his locker. He was clad in a Montreal Canadians T-shirt and a Super Bowl XXXII hat.

Jared looked disappointed. "He didn't wear his Stars jersey!"

"He's an All-Star now," said Alexia in disgust. "He's too important to show loyalty to the Martians."

Her brother stared at her. "What are you talking about, Lex? You didn't wear *your* jersey, either!"

"That's different," she said righteously. "I'm not wearing mine because I happen to think Spirit Day is stupid."

"Maybe Trent thinks that, too," I suggested.

She made a face. "Then why does he have a part in the big assembly this afternoon?"

Josh rolled his eyes. "The assembly is to honor sports achievements and to cheer on the All-Stars in the tournament."

"What we're doing this weekend is way better than being on any All-Star team!" Jared enthused. "We get to watch the tournament final *and* we get taken to a real NHL game!" He turned to me. "All thanks to your dad!"

I was thrilled that the team loved my father, but I had to set the record straight. "Listen, Jared, my dad's a great guy and all that. But this trip is one hundred percent Boom Boom. It's his idea and his Red Wings tickets."

Talk to the wall! I knew that he hadn't heard one single word. "It's going to be amazing — streaking down the ice, and everybody can read the name on my back: 'Enoch'!" He looked at me, and his eyes were green with envy. "My dad's an accountant," he confessed. "I wish he was cool like your dad."

Cal came running up, dodging feet, hockey sticks, and book bags in the crowded hall. "You're never going to believe this!" he exclaimed excitedly. "Check it out!"

He thrust a glossy magazine into the center of our group. I gawked at the words at the top of the open page: *HOW CAN THEY SLEEP AT NIGHT?*

"It's Lex's flyer!" crowed Josh in delight.

"Trent Ruben's flyer," she corrected under her breath.

The notice was reproduced in the top corner, beside a small article. My heart was pounding as I read aloud: *"In these days of million-dollar salaries and shoe contracts, it's easy to forget the passion and fire that made us fall in love with sports in the first place. In a town with the unlikely name of Mars, kids were so outraged by a teammate's exclusion from the All-Star team that they printed hundreds of these leaflets —"*

Alexia savagely yanked the article out of Cal's hands. "What kind of a stupid magazine publishes this garbage?" she snarled, turning to the cover.

I felt my eyes bulge. It was the newest issue of *Sports Illustrated.*

I swallowed a *"Yahoo!"* so humongous I'm amazed my head didn't blast clear off my shoulders. That notice was *my writing*! And there it was in *Sports Illustrated*!

Bittersweet agony flooded all over me. I couldn't tell anybody! If Alexia found out I was behind those flyers, I was dead meat! And if the word leaked to Mrs. Spiro and Mr. Lambert — it was too terrible even to think about.

Still, there was one person I could share this amazing news with! Just before the bell, I ran to the pay phone by the office and dialed Dad's hotel. Aw, man! He wasn't in his room! I wanted to shriek this news to the four winds!

But it was impossible to stay disappointed for very long on Spirit Day. There was just too much hoopla going on.

The excitement level rose as the day wore on. By lunch, the cafeteria sounded like a pep rally. I left my tape recorder running on the bench. It picked up some pretty weird conversations: Who was better — Gordie Howe or Paul Kariya? Never mind that there were forty years between the careers of those two players. Was Wayne Gretzky as good at hockey as Michael Jordan was at basketball? And if they arm-wrestled, who would win? I actually heard some grade-five kid bet that if last year's championship Penguins grew up and played together, they could beat the Detroit Red Wings team that won the Stanley Cup.

Pretty nuts. But in a world where *I* could be published in *Sports Illustrated*, anything is possible. I tried Dad three more times during lunch. No answer.

All this craziness led up to the assembly at 2:30, where the whole school jammed into the auditorium. I sat between Josh and Jared while the cheerleaders from Waterloo High riled up the crowd.

The All-Star team was up there. And let me tell you, I know Egyptian pharaohs who were worshipped less. Mr. Lambert was making a huge deal that the famous HOT line was going to be reunited in the tournament. Trent was sandwiched between Happer and Oliver. Those two idiots had brought the league championship banner, which normally hung in the community center. They were waving it and carrying on like maniacs. Whenever possible, they made sure to stick it two inches in front of Trent's nose. The message was clear: *We're defending champions, and you're not. In your face!*

When Mr. Lambert introduced the HOT line, Happer and Oliver received standing ovations, and all

Trent got was a trickle of polite applause. There were a few catcalls in there, too, and someone even yelled, "*Mar-tian!*" That was totally unfair. Trent Ruben was a Waterloo kid as much as any of them.

Beside me, I felt Josh stiffen. "Those jerks."

I'd forgotten how much flak Trent took for being on our team. No wonder he hadn't worn his Stars shirt. He didn't want to make a bad situation worse.

Then the principal introduced Mr. Feldman, who had an announcement to make on behalf of the league.

"Unfortunately, there was a typing error on the All-Star list," the president told us, "and one name was left off. Would Alexia Colwin please stand up?"

And she did, her chin stuck out halfway to Mars. She looked like a defiant sea captain in a hurricane. Only instead of wind and rain, it was cheers and boos that whirled all around her.

Mr. Feldman cast her a frozen smile. "Congratulations, Alexia. It looks like you'll be joining the All-Stars in the tournament."

Josh, Jared, and I exchanged high fives. "It's because of *Sports Illustrated*!" I hissed. "That magazine has *power*!"

Headline ideas whipped around my head like M&M's in a blender: *Marser All-Star* or *Girl All-Star* or maybe even *It's About Time!*

Alexia waited for the gym to quiet down. In a soft voice, she said, "I'm sorry, I have to wash my hair this weekend."

Onstage, Trent leaped to his feet. "*What?!*"

That *what?* was echoed all over by me, Josh, Jared, and about a hundred other people.

Mr. Feldman was bug-eyed. "*All* weekend?" he managed finally.

Alexia nodded. "I like having really clean hair."

This news was *huge*! Nobody had ever said no to the All-Stars before, much less the only girl to make it! I practically broke my arm popping my tape machine out of my pocket. But by the time I turned it on, all I recorded was the shocked silence in the gym.

So I added a whispered note, just for me. "Buy a hundred copies of *Sports Illustrated* before it sells out!"

]]]]] *Chapter 13*

Packing on Saturday morning was tough. Since there were so many of us, we could only take one small suitcase each. Mom wanted me to waste most of my precious space on *clothes*.

"I'm a reporter, not a fashion model," I reminded her. "I don't need clean underwear. I need extra batteries for my tape recorder. And a camera with a big zoom lens."

"Well, we don't have one, Clarence. So you might as well bring underwear. You'll need a little spending money, too." She took out a twenty-dollar bill and held it just outside my reach. "First I want your promise that not one penny of this will go for jawbreakers."

"Sure, Mom." I wasn't even lying. One penny

would *not* go for jawbreakers. The other nineteen dollars and ninety-nine cents? Jawbreakers.

Dad was supposed to pick me up at ten, but I wasn't holding my breath. My father was notoriously late for stuff like this. So I was kind of surprised to hear the bell at ten o'clock on the dot.

I threw open the door. "Hi, Dad! Ready to saddle up —"

It was Boom Boom.

"Sorry, Coach. I thought you were my dad."

There was an anxious look in the praying-mantis eyes. "You mean he's not here?"

"Not yet. Why?"

The coach looked uncomfortable. "I just called his whatchamacallit. The whosis at the desk said he checked out yesterday."

Mom appeared in the hall. "Oh, hi, Boom Boom." Her eyes traveled from Boom Boom's worried face to my crestfallen one. She knew instantly. "*Don't* tell me!"

"Maybe he had to go somewhere else for one day," I babbled. "So he checked out, but he's coming back —"

"I'll phone the car rental company." Mom disappeared into the kitchen. When she came back, her expression was grave. "He dropped the van off yesterday morning," she reported. "At the airport."

"Oh, boy." Coach Bolitsky took a deep breath. "The doohickey just hit the dingus."

"But why didn't he call?" I pleaded.

My mother gave a gentle shrug. "He probably just didn't want to upset you, Clarence."

"But he *promised*!" I insisted.

"The real problem is how to get fourteen people in only two doojigs," mused Boom Boom.

Mom looked blank. "Doojigs?"

"Cars," I translated miserably. I could barely look my mother in the eye. "It's all my fault! You warned me about this! But I wouldn't listen. And now the whole trip is ruined!"

Yeah, I was mad at Dad. But mostly I was mad at myself. I knew he wasn't staying forever. But I always pictured his departure way in the future, with me and the team waving good-bye. Never in a million years did I consider that he might bail out on the trip! I felt more stupid than betrayed. It was the hip-wader thing all over again.

"The team is going to kill me!" I moaned.

"No, they won't," said Boom Boom. But even he didn't sound convinced.

"I'll drive," my mother said suddenly.

I stared at her. "I thought you had to work this weekend."

"Just let me make a couple of phone calls, and I'll fix that," she replied.

The coach's relief was obvious. "You're a thingam-abob, Lisa!"

"A lifesaver!" I translated. "And a great mom!"

We sportswriters know when someone is coming through in the clutch. What she was doing for us that day was like scoring the winning goal in the last second of quadruple overtime!

It was a really long drive from Mars to Windsor. I had a pounding headache, which the squeezing of my headband was making even worse. I would have paid a million dollars in cold, hard cash for a jaw-breaker. But with Mom at the wheel, I was traveling with my own personal police force. And it didn't help that Jared and Cal jabbered about my father for every mile.

"I can't believe he's missing the trip," mourned Cal. "This really stinks for your dad."

"He's an unlucky guy," I agreed miserably.

Jared was distraught. "What am I going to do without Mr. Adelman? I was just starting to get really good at batting down the puck. He helped me so much!"

"I'm sure he'd want you to keep practicing, Jared," my mom murmured absently.

Josh, our other passenger, was a lot sharper than Cal or Jared. I think he figured out that Dad had taken off on us without a backward glance. All he said was, "I'm sorry, Chipmunk."

Cal was relentless. "I guess he'll bring us the names for our jerseys when he comes back."

"You know, Cal," Mom began carefully, "Mr. Adelman is a pretty busy person. I'm not sure you can count on seeing him anytime soon."

"Oh, I get it." Jared nodded wisely. "He's going to have to mail them to us."

When it comes to chains of thought, poor Jared couldn't work up a charm bracelet.

All three cars stopped for a break at a service area on the highway. We got drinks, and Mrs. B. passed out Mallomars for everybody.

Man, did I ever need something sweet! I took a humongous bite. Tofu.

We all made a beeline for the bathroom, and the Mallomars got a burial at sea.

"Too bad Trent isn't here," commented Brian. "He's the only one who likes this stuff."

Kyle laughed. "Maybe tofu makes you an All-Star."

"Nah," said Josh. "Lex made the team, and she

never touches the stuff. Guaranteed she's in the ladies' room next door doing exactly the same thing."

"I will *never* understand your sister," said Cal. "If I ever won a spot on the All-Star team, I would be there, like, yesterday!"

Josh shrugged. "So would everybody. But Lex isn't everybody. If they'd picked her the first time, she'd be with them now. But they didn't. And that was their one chance."

Most of the players switched cars for the rest of the drive. Jared and Cal won the coin toss, so they got to ride with Mrs. Bolitsky. Josh went off to join Boom Boom on the Doohickey Express. Brian, Kyle, and Mike squeezed in with me and Mom. So now I had to listen to those three guys talk about how sorry they felt for "poor Mr. Adelman" because he had to miss our trip.

We got to Windsor around three-thirty and went to check into our hotel. We were staying at the same place as the sixteen All-Star teams, so the lobby was tournament headquarters. There were giant bulletin boards with all the stats from the games.

The results of today's semifinals were just being posted. The team from Kent County League had won their game. That was no surprise. Kent County were last year's champions, and here they were in the final again. And —

"We won!" piped up Cal.

We all cheered. There it was — Waterloo 5, Middletown 2. Okay, there were no Marsers on the team. But at least, in the final tomorrow, we could root for Trent.

I took out my tape machine and began recording some of the stats from the big board. Trent was the leading scorer of the whole tournament, with seven goals and five assists in only three games. He'd be a shoo-in for MVP with twelve points. That was six more than second place — I frowned — Happer Feldman. Third place? My heart sank. Oliver Witt.

The headline was so obvious. Even a lousy sportswriter would think of it: *HOT Line on Fire!*

But I couldn't bring myself to say it out loud.

"Wow." That was from Josh. I looked around, and it was obvious that everyone was thinking the same thing, even our dumb guys. The Stars were working hard and getting better. But on their best day, they were still holding Trent back. Now, reunited with his old linemates from the Penguins, he was dominating the tournament.

"I guess we've seen the last of Trent Ruben," Alexia said dryly. "He's sure not going to want to come back to us after this performance."

"He's our teammate," Josh protested weakly.

"Our good friend Mr. Feldman can fix that," she

replied sourly. "And the way he's been playing, who's going to say no to the glorious Trent Ruben?"

Boom Boom appeared with a handful of hotel keys. "Break up into pairs. We're staying two to a whatchamacallit."

"Two to a room," translated his wife. "Let's drop off our stuff and meet back here in ten minutes."

‖‖‖‖ _Chapter 14_

Coach Bolitsky had a few errands to run before dinner. So Mom and Mrs. B. took us on a tour of Detroit.

Windsor and Detroit are right across the river from each other — sort of like Mars and Waterloo, only larger. Even Windsor is a lot bigger than Waterloo. And Detroit is humongous.

We Marsers don't get a lot of chances to see big cities. So we had a really good time looking at the tall buildings and the crowds of people, and cheering along with the honking of horns. We got the most psyched about stuff city people don't think twice about — taxis, parking meters, police sirens, window washers a million miles up a skyscraper. You don't see that in Mars, where the tallest building is Cal's house.

Boom Boom met us for dinner, which was at a Greek restaurant downtown. And then came the best part of all — the Red Wings game.

Just walking inside the Joe Louis Arena made me think of the long hockey tradition in this city — from the great Gordie Howe right on up to the stars of today, like Steve Yzerman and Sergei Fedorov.

I would have been impressed if our seats had been in the last row, behind a pole. But when I found out that Coach Bolitsky had arranged for us to sit in the press box — the *press box!* — I flipped out.

"Just like the real reporters!" I howled. I threw myself in the door like I was being shot out of a cannon. Even though the game hadn't started yet, I pressed my nose up against the glass and stared down at the deserted ice surface. "This is so cool!"

From beside me, a gravelly voice said, "Hey, kid, you're smearing the window. Some of us have to work here, you know."

"I'm working, too," I told the rumpled older man in the chair beside me. "I'm reporting on this game for the *Waterloo Elementary School Gazette.*"

"Waterloo?" He sounded interested. "Isn't that the town where they won't let a girl on the All-Star team?"

I was thrilled. "You read about us in *Sports Illustrated?*"

"Kid, I *wrote* that article. I'm the hockey writer for *S.I.*" He stuck out a big paw. "Dan Flockhart."

I was completely dazzled as we shook hands. "But how did you get the flyer? Did one blow all the way to your house?"

He laughed. "I showed up for work one morning, and there it was on my fax machine. I can't remember who it came from. Mitch Somebody."

Dad! Wasn't that just like him? Who else could be so awful and so fantastic, all in the same week?

"It was perfect timing," Mr. Flockhart went on. "Deadline day, and I had writer's block."

I watched as a very familiar bulge in his cheek shifted from one side to the other. Except for the beard, it was like looking in a mirror. "Is that a — a *jawbreaker*?"

He nodded. "Licorice Cannonball."

I couldn't hold it in. "Mom! It's the *Sports Illustrated* reporter! *And he eats jawbreakers!*"

"Does his dentist drive a Rolls-Royce?" she shot back. Talk about a one-track mind!

I introduced Mr. Flockhart to the team. He didn't recognize Alexia, but he was pretty sure he'd seen Cal somewhere before.

"Oh, that was me on the flyer," Cal explained proudly. "But don't worry. The rest of it was all her."

Mr. Flockhart turned out to be a terrific guy. Even

when I admitted that I was out to steal his job, he was still nice to me. I would have been happy that night if the Red Wings hadn't even shown up. But they did. And it was amazing!

We rooted for the home team. But the visitors were the Dallas Stars. So we were kind of pulling for them, too, us being fellow Stars and all that.

A 2–2 tie went into overtime. We screamed ourselves hoarse when Steve Yzerman won the game for Detroit. It was a happy crew that piled into the cars for the short drive back to Windsor.

Josh and I were roommates. We were pretty zonked, but we were too wound up to think about going to sleep.

I headed straight for the phone. "Hello, room service? Could you please send an extra-large platter of jawbreakers up to room 504?"

There was laughter on the other end of the line. "We don't carry jawbreakers in the restaurant, kid," came a woman's voice. "Besides, I've got a memo not to deliver anything to your block of rooms. It's signed by a Mr. Bolitsky."

Totally deflated, I put down the receiver. "I never knew the coach was such a suspicious guy," I commented.

"I'm going to call Trent," Josh decided. "You

know — to congratulate him and wish him luck in the final tomorrow."

"Good idea," I approved. While Josh was on the phone, I peered out the window, just in case there were any candy stores near the hotel. No such luck.

Josh hung up with a frown. "The desk clerk said they're still out celebrating."

I checked my watch. "It's after eleven. That must be some party."

Josh sighed. "Maybe Lex is right. Trent would be better off without us."

That thought took some of the shine off the evening. We stayed up, calling Trent's room. It was almost midnight when we finally drifted off to sleep, exhausted.

The next thing I knew, there was a loud pounding at our door. I shook myself awake just in time to hear a voice in the hall:

"Coach Bolitsky! Wake up!"

I stared at the digital clock. 1:17.

More pounding. "Come on, Coach! Wake up! It's an emergency!"

Josh and I ran to the door and threw it open.

There in the hall, wild-eyed and rumpled, was Trent Ruben.

"What's wrong?" cried Josh.

"Where's the coach?" demanded Trent.

My mom appeared, with her roommate, Alexia, in tow. "What's going on out here?" She glared at me. "For Pete's sake, Clarence. You *sleep* with that stupid headband?"

"I just came from the hospital!" Trent gasped.

"The *hospital*?" Boom Boom burst out of the end room in flowered pajamas.

"Mr. Feldman took us out for pizza!" Trent explained breathlessly. "And the whole team got food poisoning! The doctor said it was the pepperoni!"

"You don't look sick to me," said Alexia. She sounded disappointed.

"I was the only guy who didn't have pepperoni," Trent replied. "I got mine with tofu." He shrugged self-consciously. "I told you I kind of like it."

"Let me get this straight," said the coach. "All the whosises except you ate the heejazz, and now they all have whatchamacallit?"

"They're sick like dogs!" Trent confirmed.

My mother was alarmed. "Are they going to be all right?"

"Yeah, but there's no way they'll be ready to play tomorrow!"

I had just read through the tournament rules. "You'll be replaced by the highest-scoring losing team from the semifinals," I supplied.

"We're not being replaced by anybody!" cried Trent stubbornly.

"You're pretty talented, Ruben," said Alexia. "But you can't win the game by yourself. You've got no team."

"I do *so* have a team!" he insisted. "*Us!* We're all members of the Waterloo League! *We* can be the All-Star team!"

Cal and Jared had just wandered into the hall, and that was the first thing they heard.

"Us?" breathed Cal. "All-Stars? How?"

"The team got poisoned," Josh put in.

Cal and Jared stared in horror at Alexia.

"I didn't do it." She shrugged. "It was the pepperoni."

At that moment, the elevator door opened, and out staggered a very green, very shaky Mr. Feldman. "Bolitsky, I need your team!"

Boom Boom opened his mouth, and an avalanche of doohickeys poured out. "We don't have our thingamajigs! Their gizmos won't fit! We need our dinguses!"

The league president raised both arms in a plea for silence. "Don't bug me. I just had my stomach pumped."

My reporter's sense was tingling pins and needles. The greatest story of all time was taking shape right here in this hotel hallway. I had to keep it going.

"You can do this, Coach!" I insisted. "You have all the real team's sticks and equipment. Some of their skates will fit. Everyone else can rent them at the rink tomorrow —"

"It's the only way," added Mr. Feldman, swallowing what looked like a bad-tasting burp. "Otherwise they'll make us forfeit."

"And we all know how unfair *that* is," said Alexia pointedly.

Boom Boom looked around at his pajama-clad players. "What do you say, team? Do you want to be whosises?"

The answer came in a hurricane of cheers and high fives. This had *Sports Illustrated* cover story written all over it! From no Marsers on the All-Star team to a whole team of Marsers! It was like — like —

The perfect headline came to me: *The All-Mars All-Stars.*

| | | | | | Chapter 15

Alexia turned out to be exactly the same size as Happer Feldman. She wore all his equipment except for the skates, which she had to rent.

Cal was a tougher fit. He used Oliver's shoulder pads, Luke Doucette's helmet, and two nonmatching elbow guards. His big clunky feet were just the right size for Coach Monahan's skates. Cal couldn't stop laughing at Jared, who borrowed his hockey pants from King Diaper.

"Hey, Jared, are they Huggies or Pampers?"

Lennox Kerr's goalie pads went up to Josh's chin, but otherwise our netminder was pretty comfortable. And skinny Mike had the smallest head in the entire Waterloo Slapshot League. Boom Boom had to stuff a bath towel in the red helmet (Terry Compton's) to keep it from falling off. When Mike stood up, ready for action, he looked like a candy apple.

Kyle fit perfectly into Willis Gerard's gear, even the skates. Unfortunately, Willis didn't have a rearview mirror attached to his face guard. Mrs. Bolitsky superglued her makeup compact onto the mask, so our reverse-defenseman was back in the business of backing up.

None of the Stars were prepared to play hockey on this trip, so they wore regular clothes under their uniforms. Cal had on a starched white dress shirt, which was the only thing left in his suitcase. A lace collar peeked out from under the neck of Alexia's All-Star jersey. Kyle wore his pajama top because he didn't have anything else with long sleeves. Jared's uniform concealed a heavy sweatshirt, complete with a front pouch and a hood that bunched up behind his neck in a big lump. He looked like the Hunchback of Notre Dame.

The locker room crackled with tension. I mean, the Stars were thrilled to be playing this game. But scared? Don't ask.

Josh put everybody's feelings into words. "How can we beat those guys? They're All-Stars, the best of the best in their league! We're just a regular team, and" — he shrugged unhappily — "and a pretty mediocre one at that."

"We're not even five hundred anymore," mourned Kyle.

"*Mediocre?*" Trent was outraged. "Don't talk like that! We're the Stars!"

"Oh, shut up, hotshot!" seethed Alexia. "We may be Martians, but we can read a stat sheet. You only need us right now because the rest of the HOT line is too busy throwing up."

"The HOT line?" I thought Trent would blow smoke out of his nose. "I can't *stand* the HOT line! I hated every minute I was stuck with Happer and Oliver! Listen, there is *no one* I'd rather play with than you guys! I may not be a genius, but I know who my friends are!"

Jared took a deep breath. "I'd feel a lot better if Mr. Adelman was here."

Boom Boom snapped his fingers. "I almost forgot. These came today."

He dumped out a box on the training table. I gawked. I goggled. It was the names! The names for the Stars' jerseys! They were brilliantly lettered in white silk against a green background that matched the Stars' uniform color.

I stared at Boom Boom. "My dad sent these?"

The coach grinned. "They were waiting at the check-in thingie this morning."

"Three cheers for Mr. Adelman!" bellowed Jared.

During the hip-hip-hoorays, there was a stampede as the players fished for their names. I couldn't take my eyes off the embroidered strips: ENOCH; AZEVEDO; A. COLWIN; J. COLWIN; RUBEN — they were gorgeous! But the really beautiful part was that Dad had come through for the team.

"Too bad we can't wear them," Josh said wistfully.

Mrs. B. stepped forward with a big box of safety pins. "We'll sew them on our real shirts when we get home. But we can pin them on for today."

Okay, they looked a little Christmassy, with green strips on the red All-Star jerseys. But when the Waterloo team took the ice that afternoon, they were showing off their names to the world.

I practically floated up to my mother in the bleachers. "Look, Mom! Dad did it! He really did it!"

She was confused. "But how could he know the Stars would be playing today?"

What?! But I didn't have time to think about it now. They were starting to introduce the teams.

The Kent County All-Stars were first. I didn't bother taking down their names. I just referred to them as King Kong, Godzilla, Bigfoot, T. Rex — you get the picture. They were massive. The smallest of them was about the size of burly Cal. The biggest should have had his own area code from the phone company.

And then they introduced our team. What a disaster! I guess nobody told them that the real All-Stars were away somewhere, recovering from bad pepperoni.

"Number seven — Happer Feldman. Number twelve — Luke Doucette —"

Our players just stood there, waiting to hear their own names, which was never going to happen. It was like a comedy routine on *Saturday Night Live*. Titters of laughter rippled through the crowd.

The referee thought the Stars were just clowning around. "You're supposed to skate forward when you get called! What are you — a bunch of wise guys?"

"Some of us are wise girls," corrected Alexia.

"Number fourteen — Oliver Witt —"

"Come on!" the referee demanded. "Where's Oliver?"

"He has food poisoning," Brian supplied.

The referee was furious. "Okay. So you guys are too important to be introduced!"

"Number sixteen — Trent Ruben —"

For once the PA announcer was right. Trent glided forward to a standing ovation, and the referee skated away, muttering under his breath.

Then it was time for the opening face-off — Godzilla versus Trent. Trent was faster, but Godzilla

113

was so strong that he trapped Trent's stick with his own. Trent couldn't move. Alexia came in and body-checked the big center. She bounced right off.

But Godzilla was more than just brute strength. He could skate and stickhandle, and he had a slap-shot like an artillery cannon. From Josh's point of view, he must have looked like a runaway train roaring in on net.

I give our poor goalie all the credit in the world. He stood right up to the guy. And a fat lot of good it did him. Eight seconds into the game, it was 1–0 for Kent County.

Oops? Did I say 1–0? Make that 2–0. Bigfoot skated through our whole team like they were trees, planted and unmoving.

You could just see our poor players start to collapse in on themselves. Their moves were uncertain. Kent County won the scramble for every loose puck. It seemed like Josh was trying to makes saves in slow motion. When he stuck out his glove or a pad, you could tell he didn't expect to stop anything.

I reminded myself that these were the defending All-Star champs. Nobody could expect an ordinary team to beat them. But it still hurt to watch our guys playing so badly. They skated like they were wading through an ocean of hot fudge.

The guy I called King Kong put together a fantastic end-to-end rush. He swatted away checkers like they were pesky mosquitos. He faked Josh out of Lennox Kerr's jockstrap, and suddenly it was 3–0.

Right then, when I was sure things couldn't get any worse, they did. Into the arena marched the All-Star team. I mean, the *real* All-Star team, with Coach Monahan and all those Penguins. Even from across the rink they looked pretty gray. But at least they weren't throwing up anymore. I know it's disloyal to the Stars, but I honestly wondered if those pepperoni zombies might still be able to do a better job out there than their replacements.

Wouldn't you know it? Happer and Oliver took the seats right behind me. Being sick had obviously done nothing to their big mouths.

"Aw, man!" roared Happer. "They gave all my equipment to the *girl*! What a diss!"

"That's nothing!" scoffed Oliver. "Look who's got my shirt — Enoch! He's the idiot who made a puck disappear."

I couldn't let that pass. I wheeled and snapped, "Shut up, you guys! The Stars are doing you a favor here!"

At that moment, Godzilla scored again. Now it was 4–0.

"Tell your Martian friends to help somebody else next time," sneered Happer. "This is going to go down in the record books as *us*!"

Oliver grabbed my headband, pulled it back, and snapped it like a slingshot.

"Ow!" I glared into their grim faces and announced, "Fried onions! Really greasy cheeseburgers! Liver sauteed in bacon fat!"

I watched in satisfaction as their pale faces went white. Their lips disappeared, and they clutched at their stomachs. Without another word, they got up and ran for the men's room.

Okay, it was a really mean thing for me to do. But I had to stand up for the team. They sure weren't standing up for themselves.

The Stars were lucky to get out of the period down by only four goals.

In the locker room, we saw something we'd never seen before. We saw Boom Boom Bolitsky blow his stack.

"You guys are playing like a bunch of doohickeys!! You're turning this game into a thingamabob!! Haven't you got any whatchamacallit?! . . ."

It was all gibberish, but nobody needed a translation. The message was clear: Kent County was great, but they didn't even have to be. The Stars were beating themselves.

⏐⏐⏐⏐⏐ Chapter 16

The players were totally cowed. They had never seen Boom Boom go nuts before. Believe me, it's something to tell your grandchildren about. His bulging eyes were red and blazing. The elastic that held his ponytail in place had snapped, and his long hair was now loose. But it didn't hang. It stood straight out, like he'd just stuck his finger in an electric socket. His face was purple with the effort of trying to communicate.

I had my tape recorder running, waiting for coaching instructions. But they never came. Instead, Boom Boom just kept on yelling until he ran out of words. He slumped against the wall, exhausted.

"You're right, Coach," sighed Alexia. "I'm not hitting. I blew that first check and I haven't thrown one since. I'm sorry."

"Me, too," said Kyle, shamefaced. "I've been skating forward. What was I thinking?"

"I'm letting them push me around," Trent confessed. "Not anymore, Coach. That's a promise."

One by one, the Stars all spoke up and took the blame for their terrible showing.

"I was scared to go into the corners."

"I stood there like a lump and let them score."

"I was afraid I couldn't stop that big guy, so I didn't even try."

What a great coach! Without even speaking English, he'd gotten his message across to every single player.

The buzzer sounded. Boom Boom still didn't have any words, so he just opened the door and pointed out toward the ice. It was the most inspiring gesture I've ever seen. The Stars went out there all fired up.

As the captain, Alexia was the first to stand up to Kent County. On the opening shift, she made another try at bodychecking Godzilla. And again she bounced off like a Ping-Pong ball. But I noticed something different. When she got up, her chin was stuck out in determination. She just kept at it — shoulder checks, hip checks, physical play. And eventually she ran into one of those guys at just the right angle.

It was T. Rex on an all-out rush. Her hip check was low. But when she felt the puck-handler leave his feet, she straightened up and finished the hit with her shoulder. T. Rex went flying.

Alexia's effort was contagious. Trent started stick-handling. And, yeah, they took the puck away from him. But each time he held it a little bit longer, and we had a few rushes. The wingers dug in the corners, and soon Waterloo had its very first shot on goal. We even got a few cheers, mostly from the real Waterloo All-Stars, who were scattered throughout the bleachers.

"They're getting better," said Oliver sourly.

"They stink!" scoffed Happer. "They're going to get shut out."

I turned to them. "Lasagna," I purred. "French onion soup. Eggs fried in butter."

They didn't have to run for the bathroom this time, but they both looked really queasy. Anyway, I'm glad they were around to see the Stars' first goal.

Okay, it was kind of by accident. But it was still a great moment. Ten minutes into the period, Kyle finally got his stick on the puck. With a whoosh, he whipped around and started on a backwards rush.

The Kent county players got confused. Whose job was it to check this guy? And just how would you do that exactly, when the puck was on the wrong side of him? Before they could decide, Kyle was coming in on net.

"*Hit him!*" shouted their goalie, Frankenstein.

Two big defensemen sandwiched Kyle right in front of the crease. The double check was so hard that a little cloud of makeup powder rose from Mrs. B.'s compact and puffed into the goalie's face.

"*A-choo!*"

And while Frankenstein was bent over sneezing, Kyle managed to poke the puck into the net.

I cheered out my headline idea: "*Waterloo Gets on the Board!*"

Happer had a slightly different headline: "*Luck. Dumb Luck.*"

I wheeled to face him. "Jalapeño chili nachos."

When Godzilla took a tripping penalty a minute later, I could really see this game starting to turn around. A power-play goal would make the score 4–2, and we had the whole third period to mount a comeback.

I could feel beads of sweat dripping down from my headband. The Stars' powerplay looked sharp. Brian and Kyle controlled the blue line, feeding Trent and Alexia. Cal worked the corners, picking up rebounds and loose pucks.

Alexia shot! Stick save, Frankenstein!

Trent took a backhand! Frankenstein got his pad in the way!

Cal corralled the puck behind the net and tried a wraparound. But the big goalie slammed his skate against the post, and the shot caromed high.

It came down right on the stick of Godzilla, who was chugging up-ice at top speed. Scrambling to get in his way, Kyle and Brian smashed into each other. Their helmets bonked together, and they fell to the ice. There was just enough space between them for the Kent center to skate through on a clean break-away.

As much as I hated it, I had to admit it was a beautiful goal. Talk about confidence. Godzilla was barely past our blue line when he shot — a blistering drive that beat Josh between the legs. 5-1, Kent County.

A shorthanded goal! There's nothing more demor-alizing than getting scored on right in the middle of your own power play. And just when it seemed like the Stars were climbing back into this game!

The locker room between periods was a very quiet place. The Stars were devastated.

"We can't beat these guys," mourned Josh. "They're ten times better than us."

"They belong in the NHL," Brian agreed.

Even Trent was shaken. "The problem is that any

one of them is good enough to take the puck all the way and score." He shook his head. "Think about it. They've got five goals, and every single one came on a huge individual effort. I'll bet there isn't an assist on the whole team."

Boom Boom stared at him. The praying-mantis eyes began to whirl. "That's it!" he crowed finally. "That's our thingamajig!"

The whole team came to attention.

"Those whosises are better than us," the coach explained, "but only one at a time! They don't pass to each other. They just make individual whatcha-macallits."

Alexia jumped to her feet. "Why didn't we think of it sooner?" she said softly. "They're showboats. They're used to *getting* passes, not *giving* them."

Cal got really excited. "So if we force them to pass, they'll start making mistakes!" He looked completely blank. "How do we do that, Coach?"

"Tight checking!" Boom Boom answered immediately.

"Right!" cheered Trent. "Don't let them skate. Throw them off their game. They'll *have* to pass!"

The Stars were so anxious to get back on the ice that they almost trampled me at the buzzer. I started for my seat, but Trent grabbed me by the collar.

"Wait a minute, Chipmunk. I've got a little job for you."

"Anything, Trent!" I vowed. I was so wrapped up in this game, I would have been willing to go spelunking in the sewer if it would help the Stars.

He put an arm around my shoulders and whispered so that the coach wouldn't hear. "There's one more thing that might throw those guys off their game."

I was all ears. "What?"

He winked. "Mrs. Bolitsky."

Chapter 17 \l\l\l\l\l

Talking to Mrs. Bolitsky is a lot harder than it looks. Just standing there in the bleachers, gazing at that supermodel face, that long black hair, those eyes — oh, don't get me started! The point is, I climbed all the way up there, took one look at Mrs. B., and forgot the plan.

"Uh — how's it going?" I babbled.

Mom jolted me back to Earth. "Clarence, do you have a fever? Your face is all flushed."

"Oh," I managed. "I'm fine. I'm just a little off my game —"

The plan!

"Mrs. Bolitsky," I announced, "Coach needs you on the bench."

She was surprised. "What for?"

I tried to look vague. "He mentioned something about doohickeys. Come on, let's go."

She followed me down the stairs. Believe me, no one in that section watched the opening face-off.

Down at ice level, she climbed onto the bench beside her husband. "What is it, Boom Boom?"

"What's what?" he asked her.

"What do you need me for?"

"Nothing."

"But, Boom Boom —"

At that moment, Bigfoot got his first look at Mrs. Bolitsky. *Crash!* He skated straight into the glass.

Kyle picked up the puck and reversed at top speed down the ice. I could see him frowning into his makeup mirror as he looked for defenders. There weren't any. The Kent County players stood flat-footed, staring at our bench. Kyle head-manned the puck to Cal, who found Mike for a shovel shot into the top corner. 5–2.

Mrs. B. joined in the celebration and then said, "Well, since nobody needs me down here —"

"Mrs. B.!" piped up Trent. "The name is falling off the back of my jersey! Please fix the safety pins, okay?"

While that was going on, King Kong leaned so far over the boards for a good view that he tumbled off the bench and onto the rink. The whistle blew.

"That's a penalty against Kent," called the referee. "Too many men on the ice."

Well, we had to keep the coach's wife down there for the power play, right? "Ow! I've got something in my eye!" I cried.

And while she dabbed at me with a Q-Tip, Frankenstein was watching her and not the puck. Brian sliced in from the point, and with a clumsy little flip shot the score was 5–3.

The Kent County coach called a time-out. When he asked his players what was wrong, they all pointed at Mrs. Bolitsky.

He looked disgusted. "*She's* the reason you're so distracted? Shame on you!" He proceeded to diagram a play on his candy bar and take a bite out of his clipboard.

When the game resumed, the defending All-Star champions kept their eyes on the ice. It took their minds off Mrs. B., but it also set them up for some of the most crushing body checks I've ever seen. I couldn't believe it! The Stars were knocking those giants all over the rink. And not just our big hitters, either. Skinny Mike sent Godzilla himself careening backwards into Frankenstein. The two of them ended up in a heap in the Kent County net.

Unable to skate without getting clobbered, Kent started passing. That's when we found out that

Boom Boom was right. These unbelievable super-stars, these hockey-playing machines, were the lousiest passers on the face of the earth.

Pretty soon, Trent intercepted a feed from King Kong to T. Rex and blasted it past Frankenstein. 5–4. Then Brian picked off a real dribbler and got it to Kyle for a backwards rush. Kyle's shot missed, but Cal was there to knock in the rebound.

"*It's all tied up!*" I howled into my tape recorder. "What a comeback!"

Boom Boom called time-out to give his exhausted players a chance to rest. His voice was hoarse from screaming, which made it even more difficult to understand him.

"There's only a minute and a half left in the whatsit!" he croaked. "Kill off the time so we can save our strength and win it in whatchamacallit!"

Trent looked horrified. "In *overtime*? Coach, there *is* no overtime in All-Star play!"

"No way!" exclaimed Jared. "You mean they just let the whole thing end in a tie?"

Trent shook his head. "When it's a tie, the trophy goes to the team with the most total goals! And Kent County scored more than Waterloo in this tournament!"

Josh flipped up his goalie mask. "Are you telling me that —"

"We're still losing," his sister supplied in reverse volume control.

"Right," Trent confirmed. "If we can't win this game in regulation time, we come in second."

Talk about drama! It all came down to a minute and a half — do-or-die. Moments like this happen only in hockey.

Mrs. Bolitsky sure wasn't leaving the bench now! The arena rang with screams, some urging the Stars to complete their miracle, others begging Kent County to hang on. I was really impressed to see some of our biggest enemies cheering for us. Luke Doucette, Terry Compton, and Lennox Kerr were up on shaky legs, yelling their support. Even Coach Monahan and Mr. Feldman seemed pretty excited.

But not Happer and Oliver. Those rotten jerks were so nasty that they were shouting their lungs out — *for the other team!* They would rather see Waterloo lose than allow any glory to go to the Marsers. How mean can you get?

I wheeled to face those two traitors and announced, "Cheese blintzes with sour cream!"

I guess they were completely recovered because that didn't gross them out at all. Oliver reached forward to yank my headband again. I tried to pull away, and the darn thing snapped right off in his hand. It sailed straight up in the air and came down on the ice, just inside the Waterloo blue line.

I shouted, "Oh, *no* —!"

But at that moment, the puck was dropped.

Trent won the draw and fired it into the Kent end. That was the signal for Josh to get off the ice so we could replace him with a sixth attacker. He scrambled for the bench. Suddenly, he was flat on his face. I goggled. He had tripped over *my headband*!

"*Get up!*" bellowed Boom Boom.

Tired, and dressed in Lennox's oversized pads, Josh wasn't moving very fast.

King Kong emerged with the puck from the scramble behind his own net. He took careful aim and fired a slapshot down the center of the rink.

A gasp went up in the arena. The drive was headed straight for the empty Waterloo net.

With a cry of purpose, Josh hurled himself sideways along the blue line, straining desperately to make a play. The sure goal whacked into the tip of his stick and deflected into the neutral zone.

"Last minute of play in the game," came the PA announcement.

Both teams stampeded after the loose puck. Josh was right out there with them, skating like a forward in his clumsy pads.

"Don't go over the heejazz!" Boom Boom bellowed at Josh.

"The red line!" I howled in translation. It's a penalty for the goalie to cross center ice.

But Josh didn't hear. His right skate reached for the line.

Wham! Alexia flung herself at her brother, knocking him backwards. The force of the hit sent him spinning, flat on the ice, over his own blue line and out of danger.

I turned anguished eyes on the clock. Thirty seconds!

Trent picked up the puck, but a slicing poke-check knocked it away from him. Brian raced for it, but so did Godzilla. Their flailing sticks met at the puck. Two separate golf shots became one. The puck soared high in the air.

All at once, there was total silence in the arena. Two teams and three hundred spectators held their breath. Deep in my sportswriter's heart, I knew that where the puck came down would determine the outcome of this tournament.

And then a voice called out, *"I got it!"*

||||| _Chapter 18_

I goggled. The voice belonged to Jared Enoch.

In silhouette against the arena lights, he looked like Michael Jordan in full flight — Air Jared, leaping for the great-granddaddy of all bat-downs.

"It's too high!" I shrieked.

But Jared had been waiting for this moment for weeks — practicing, slaving, perfecting his technique. He stretched open the fingers of his hockey glove and knocked the puck out of the sky.

It came down at an angle and bounced off the side of Bigfoot's helmet. As though aimed by an evil spirit, it did a little flip and disappeared down the neckband of Jared's All-Star jersey.

"Oh, no!" wailed Jared. "Not again!" His skates crunched back down onto the ice, and he did a mad howling dance, arms pounding away at his uniform.

Fifteen seconds left in the game! The referee began to raise his arm to whistle the play dead. But suddenly, the puck dropped out of Jared's shirt and hit the ice. It rolled through a tangle of eager sticks and right up to Trent.

"*Go-o-o-o!!*" I yowled, with one eye on the ice and the other on the clock. 9 — 8 — 7 —

But this was the great Trent Ruben. He knew exactly how much time he had as he swooped in on net. With three seconds left, he fired a perfect wrist shot at the bottom corner.

Clang!

"*He hit the post!*" I wheezed in agony. *No!* To come so far just to lose by a clang —

Then I saw Alexia. She flew out of nowhere, her body parallel to the ice in a desperation dive. She took a wild swing, and the heel of her stick caught the rebound.

Frankenstein lunged for it and missed. The puck slid under him, and the red goal light flashed on a split second before the clock ticked down to zero.

Final score: 6–5 for the All-Mars All-Stars, tournament champions.

We didn't have that many fans in the arena. But we screamed loud enough to make up for it. Man, in the Red Wings game last night, I don't think a crowd of eighteen thousand cheered any louder. They definitely weren't any happier.

Boom Boom and the team stormed the ice, and I was hot on their heels. They picked Alexia up on their shoulders and carried her off into the locker room. But any decent reporter has a sense of drama. I slip-slid along the ice and fished the game-winning puck out of the net. Now every time we looked at it, we could relive the greatest moment in the short history of Mars hockey.

Holding it high, I ran into a locker room that was joyous bedlam. I marched right up and held it out to the player who deserved it most of all.

"Here," I said to Alexia. "You'll want to save this."

She didn't even look at it. She was staring at my face. "Chipmunk," she said, "how come it says 'Copymax' on your forehead?"

Oh, no! In all the excitement, I'd forgotten that my headband was gone!

You could almost see Alexia's mind working like a computer. My bruise . . . the Copymax copier . . . where the flyers . . .

Her eyes narrowed. "It was *you!* Those stupid papers! *You* printed them!"

Wouldn't you know it? Here, at the moment of greatest happiness, I was going to get bodychecked into a pulp.

"Go ahead!" I challenged. "Beat me up! I still think I did the right thing!"

Alexia looked amazed. "You did all that for me? That was really sweet, Chipmunk. Thanks."

Trent leaped up from his seat beside her on the bench. "Sweet? *Sweet?* When you thought it was me, you made me eat one of those flyers!"

Alexia grinned. "Here, hotshot. Play with this." She handed him the winning puck.

He frowned at it. "Wait a minute. This isn't the right puck."

"Sure it is," I insisted. "I picked it up out of the net."

"But the tournament pucks have the All-Star crest. This one —" He held it out to me. *WSL* was scratched into the rubber. "This is a Waterloo Slap-shot League puck!"

"Let me see that thingamajig!" exclaimed Boom Boom. He grabbed it, bewildered. "How did this get here?"

Brian stared in wonder. "Hey, you don't think this could be the puck Jared lost way back in the Kings' game?"

"That's impossible!" Jared shouted. "That puck totally disappeared! And even if it didn't, how could it be *here*, hundreds of miles away from home? You think I carried it in my belly button?"

To illustrate his point, he slapped his stomach. A strange look came over his face. "You know, there's something in here!" He lifted up his jersey to reveal the kangaroo pocket of his hooded sweatshirt. He reached inside and pulled out a puck.

Kyle pointed. "This one has the All-Star crest!"

"I knew it!" Brian exclaimed. "I told you that old puck was stuck in the laundry somewhere! It rolled into that pocket and got packed in your suitcase for Windsor!"

Jared was plainly awestruck. "And it scored the winning goal!" he breathed.

Trent's brow furrowed. "That's a good point, Coach," he said to Boom Boom. "Technically, the real puck disappeared, and the one we scored with was from outside the game. By the rules, that goal shouldn't count."

Alexia cast him a withering glare. "One puck went into Jared's shirt, and one puck came out. Who cares which puck?"

Josh looked worried. "What should we do, Coach?"

At that instant, the locker room door swung wide, and in stepped Mr. Feldman. The league president was carrying the gleaming All-Star trophy.

In a lightning motion, Boom Boom crammed the illegal puck into his mouth, closed his lips over it, and did his best to smile like the winning coach.

I was blown away! He must have a cavern back there!

"Well, Bolitsky," said Mr. Feldman, handing over the trophy, "I take my hat off to you. I admit I had my doubts, but your Martians — uh — players really showed something out there. Have you got a comment for the league newsletter?"

"Uh-uh," mumbled Boom Boom, his face bursting.

Since I was the team reporter, I felt that I should be in charge of quotes. "Just put that we're thrilled to be here," I beamed.

He didn't write it down. He just stood there, staring at me. Not into my eyes, but somewhere above them.

"Young man, why does it say 'Copymax' on your face?"

Oh, boy.

ⅠⅠⅠⅠⅠ *Chapter 19*

Mr. Feldman ratted me out to the school over the flyers. I got suspended for two days. I would have preferred to be suspended until Mr. Sarkis retired. But I figured I could just steer clear of him until graduation.

In a way, I got off easy. Alexia didn't kill me, and the team thought I was a hero. Even Mom was kind of proud that I stood up for a teammate, especially a girl. Who cares what Mr. Feldman thought?

Anyway, the two days gave me the time to finish up my post-tournament interviews and prepare my report for the next *Gazette*.

I interviewed Mrs. Bolitsky last, since it's so hard to concentrate when she's around. I picked a good time. She was busy at her desk, paying some of the bills for Mars Health Food. She only smiled at me once. I got so flustered that I fell off my chair. But that turned out to be a good thing. While I was down there, I found a receipt she had dropped. Honest, I didn't mean to snoop. But my reporter's instinct has a mind of its own.

The invoice was from a company called Windsor Athletic Uniforms. It said that a Mr. B. Bolitsky had bought eleven custom name patches (white on green). It was dated the day before the All-Star final — rush order.

My heart gave an extra ba-bump. The names for the jerseys! This meant they had come from Boom Boom. Not only that, but our coach was letting me and everybody else believe that my father had sent them.

Have I ever mentioned that Boom Boom was the greatest guy in the world? Well, triple it. He bought those name strips because he didn't want the team to be disappointed. *And* he let Dad have all the credit because he knew how uncomfortable I felt about my father running out on us the way he did.

"What have you got there, Chipmunk?"

I handed her the fallen receipt. Our eyes locked. "Oh, Mrs. Bolitsky," I managed. "I've got to tell the team about this!"

"That's not what Boom Boom wants," she said sharply.

"Everybody should know what a fantastic thing he did," I insisted.

But she made me promise to keep the secret. I wasn't even allowed to tell Boom Boom that *I* knew.

I did tell Dad, though, when he called a week later. He agreed with me that Boom Boom was a pretty special guy.

With a mouth big enough to hide an eighteen-wheeler, I thought. Out loud I said, "I know you're the one who sent my flyer to *Sports Illustrated*. It was a dream come true. Thanks."

"At your service." There was an uncomfortable silence on the other end of the line. Then, "What an amazing All-Star weekend it turned out to be! I'm really sorry I had to miss it, Chipmunk."

I stopped myself just short of saying, "That's okay." Because it wasn't okay. But I really didn't feel mad at him anymore. It was just Dad being Dad. Making a big stink would be like yelling at a compass because it refused to point south.

"Anyway, it all worked out," I told him.

"Hey, Chipmunk," he chuckled. "How's my buddy Jared doing? Did he ever learn how to bat down a puck?"

"Oh, Dad!" Now it was my turn to laugh. "Someday, when you've got about a month, I'll tell you all about it. It was a supernatural event of the unexplained!"

Look for Slapshots #3

The Battle of the Doohickeys

Mrs. Spiro was not pleased when she found out about our egg babies. The whole team, except for Jared, had to stay after school in — you guessed it — the art room. While we were blowing yolk into paper towels, Mrs. Spiro gave us a lecture about "taking this project a little more seriously."

Personally, I don't believe real babies are as delicate as eggshells. If they were, very few of us would live to grow up. Mrs. Spiro probably never thought of that.

The weekend hockey results were on everyone's lips. The big news was that the Oilers had won again. They destroyed the Panthers 6–0 yesterday — a huge upset. The new kid, Steve Stapleton, scored four goals and assisted on the other two.

Alexia painted the finishing touches of a space helmet on her new egg baby, Sally (named after Sally Ride, the astronaut). She shot Trent a dazzling smile. "Could there be a new hotshot in town?" She loved razzing Trent.

Her co-captain wasn't taking the bait. "Guys like Steve Stapleton get people interested in junior hockey," he said seriously. "He'll be good for the league — you know, if he's as talented as everybody thinks."

"He won't be good for the goalies," put in Josh,

placing Dominic II in his shoe box. "What if he scores fifty on me?"

"We're going to find out," his sister told him. "We play the Oilers in the last game of the season."

That wasn't soon enough for me. No way could the *Gazette* sports reporter wait until the end of the year to get a look at the biggest news story in the league.

That's why I was rushing to get this egg degunked. The Oilers were practicing at the community center right now. It was the perfect chance for me to watch Steve Stapleton play, and maybe even interview him afterward.

"Don't blow so hard, Clarence," Mrs. Spiro admonished me. "You don't want to hurt her."

"Her?" I repeated.

"Maybe you'd be a little more careful if you had a baby girl to look after," she suggested.

"Great idea, Mrs. Spiro." (Dumb idea, Mrs. Spiro.)

I reached for the pink paint — you know, more feminine and all that. The face got kind of smudged. Either that or my "daughter" had two noses. Hey, I was in a hurry!

Mrs. Spiro sighed. "All right, Clarence. What's her name?"

Well, how could I look at something round and

pink without dreaming of Ultra Quarks, the most delicious jawbreakers ever invented? They taste like a real peanut-butter-and-jelly sandwich!

"Her name is Quark," I told her.

"Quark?" she repeated. "She's a little girl! What kind of a name is Quark?"

But I was already running down the hall, the shoe box tucked in the crook of my arm like a football.

I made it to the community center in time to catch the last ten minutes of the Oilers' workout. "Stapleton practice, March 7," I dictated into my tape recorder. "Steve is number —"

It took about a millionth of a second to spot him. Number 12. He wasn't bigger than the rest of the guys, but he was more heavily built. The other Oilers looked like first-graders in comparison. And *balance* — the whole team couldn't knock him off the puck.

"He moves like his skates are part of his feet," I recorded.

I watched him fake out five guys and score. His shot was a bullet — accurate and deadly. It was like someone had taken a real professional and plopped him down right in the middle of the Waterloo Slapshot League.

Man, was this guy news! It was the biggest story

since Trent got kicked off the Penguins and sent over to the Stars.

I skulked around outside the locker room after the practice, brainstorming questions to ask Steve. Hockey stuff — you know, about his style, and what NHL players he admired.

The door opened, and Ned Gallagher, the Oilers' captain, stepped out. He took one look at my shoe box and snorted a laugh at me. "Quark? Hey, Chipmunk — is it your egg baby or your science project?"

Ned was a good guy — sort of a class-clown type. He was in grade seven, so he was done with the egg-baby part of life, lucky him.

"Is Steve Stapleton coming out soon?" I asked.

He looked suspicious. "Why?"

I shrugged. "I have to interview him."

"Oh, don't bother Steve," Ned said airily. "I can tell you everything you need to know."

"Well, I suppose we could start that way," I offered reluctantly. I clicked on my tape recorder. "How long has he been playing hockey?"

"Forever," Ned replied. "A really long time. Not *that* long," he interrupted himself. "Just — long."

You know how Spider-Man has spider sense? Well, I have the same kind of thing — not spider, obviously, but a sixth sense for reporters. Whenever there's a news story hiding somewhere, my reporter's sense tingles. Right now it was zapping me like a dentist's drill with no novocaine.

When the other Oilers began to emerge, every single one of them had something to add to my interview. Pretty soon there were seven or eight guys out there telling me who Steve's favorite player was.

"Mark Messier."

"Jaromir Jagr."

"Wayne Gretzky."

"Joe Sakic."

Four Oilers gave me four names.

I frowned. "Well, which one is it?"

They started again. This time they listed four *different* players.

"Why don't we ask Steve himself?" I suggested. "He should be coming out any minute."

And they all started babbling about how Steve can't be disturbed. Why? Was he performing open heart surgery?

I clicked off the recorder. "I'm going to wait for Steve."

Eventually, they left me alone. But they hung around the snack bar. I could tell they were watching me.

One of the bad things about the great job of reporting is that there's a lot of waiting. It took *twenty minutes* for Steve to emerge.

The first thing I noticed about him was his neck. He didn't have one. His head was connected to his shoulders by muscles. Lots of them.

I hit *record*. "Hey, Steve, how about answering a few questions for the *Gazette*?"

His clear blue eyes narrowed. "For the what?" His voice was way down there — really deep.

"The Waterloo Elementary School Gazette," I explained. "I'm the sports reporter, Chipmunk Adelman."

He frowned. "What kind of a name is Chipmunk?" Below bass.

I flashed him my chipmunk face, making the ball in my cheek with my tongue. "I used to have a jawbreaker problem."

"Well, I have an interview problem," he informed me. "I'm a really shy guy, okay? Nothing personal." And he turned his broad back on me and walked away.

Some athletes have a stormy relationship with the press.

I watched him wade into the crowd of high-fiving teammates at the snack bar. He was laughing and slapping right along with them. Shy, eh? He looked about as shy as a tiger shark.

"He's hiding something," I whispered into my tape recorder.

Cautiously, I edged over. The Oilers were fighting over who was going to get to buy Steve a hot chocolate. I looked at the pile of sports bags in the middle of the floor. Steve's was the red one. Now, I'm not a snoop, but when you're a reporter, you train yourself to notice stuff. Things a detective might pick up — details, clues, *unzipped red duffel bags!*

I can't help it. My eyes have a nose for news. I strolled over casually and peered inside at Steve's gear. He had the usual hockey equipment in there — skates, gloves, pads, and *aha*!

A large tube of pancake makeup.

Makeup? Hockey players don't wear makeup! He was covering something. But what? A scar? Tons of athletes have them. A pimple? Big deal. I had to see for myself.

Tucking my shoe box under my arm, I pushed through the crowd up to Steve. When he turned his head, I dropped to the floor and pretended to tie my shoe. From my squat position, I craned my neck to get a perfect worm's-eye view of him. And there was the makeup, just as I suspected —

"You again?!" Rough hands grabbed me by the collar. I was yanked to my feet where I came face to very angry face with Steve Stapleton. "Kid," he rumbled, "when I say no interviews, I mean no interviews!"

"But —" I protested.

He gave me a little shove. "Get out of here!"

I went flying. As I staggered back, I stepped on my shoe box. My foot broke right through the lid.

Crack!

"Oh, no!" I peeked inside. Being a girl hadn't helped Quark. She was in about twenty pink pieces.

But my heart was soaring. Another busted eggshell was a small price to pay for solving the riddle of the mysterious Steve Stapleton.

About the Author

"When I played hockey as a kid, one of the biggest deals was getting to be an All-Star," Gordon Korman remembers. "We spent hours discussing who made it, who didn't, and why. So when I was writing the Slapshots series, it hit me — would the league pick any 'Martians' for the All-Star team? No way! But I was pretty sure Chipmunk and the Stars wouldn't take this lying down!"

Gordon Korman has written more than twenty books for middle-grade and young adult readers, among them *Liar, Liar, Pants on Fire; The Chicken Doesn't Skate; Why Did the Underwear Cross the Road?; The Toilet Paper Tigers;* seven books in the popular Bruno and Boots series; and most recently Slapshots #1: *The Stars from Mars*, all published by Scholastic. He lives with his wife and their son in Great Neck, New York.